The
GINGERBREAD
House

Kate Beaufoy also writes as Kate Thompson. *The Gingerbread House* is her fifteenth novel. Her last – *Another Heartbeat in the House* – was shortlisted for the Irish Book Awards. A former actress, Kate has an MA in English and French from Trinity College, Dublin. Kate lives some of the year in Dublin and some on the west coast of Ireland. She is an advanced-level scuba diver, a wild swimmer, a keen practitioner of Bikram yoga, and the fond keeper of a bewitching Burmese cat.

www.katebeaufoy.com

The
GINGERBREAD
House

KATE BEAUFOY

BLACK & WHITE PUBLISHING

First published 2017
by Black & White Publishing Ltd
29 Ocean Drive, Edinburgh EH6 6JL

1 3 5 7 9 10 8 6 4 2   17 18 19 20

ISBN: 978 1 78530 086 8

A CIP catalogue record for this book is available from the British Library.

For the steadfast walkers: Hilary, Malcolm, Marian, Mark and Tony.

For Ciarán, who would be with us if he could, and for Clara, who is always there in spirit.

'Real life is only one kind of life – there is also the life of the imagination.'

E.B. White, author of *Charlotte's Web*

1

How We Came to Live There

Mama cried the day she had to go to the Gingerbread House. Dad drove us there and parked the car under the cherry tree. Mama sat in the passenger seat and cried and cried while cherry blossom came drifting down, covering the windscreen in a pale blanket.

'It's only for three weeks.' Dad's trying to sound reassuring as he hands Mama another tissue. The scent of honeysuckle is coming in through the open window and I can hear a blackbird's song.

'I know. I'm being ridiculous. Three weeks is no time at all. It's just that I can't bear the idea of saying goodbye. I can't bear the idea of watching you drive away.'

The blossom continues to fall as they sit in silence. I want my parents to have these final moments to themselves, so I slip out of the car and take a wander around the garden.

The Gingerbread House is very pretty on the outside. It's washed in pale pink, and pink flowers called clematis grow around the front door and windows. It has a red tiled roof, and a sun porch, and there is garden all around – four gardens, to be precise. There is a flat lawn on one side,

1

where nothing of any interest grows, a patio garden with plants in pots and a sundial to the rear, a garden with space for parking to the front, and a secret garden.

The secret garden is my favourite. You climb up stone steps to get to it. It's so overgrown with tangled greenery that, once there, you can sit and watch out for people on the road below, knowing that they cannot see you. You could be sitting there for a long time, waiting. Not many people pass along on the road that runs past the Gingerbread House.

The isolation is going to be the killing thing . . . That's what Mama said to Dad as they drove out here. And he said *I know. I'm sorry. But at least you'll have the worldwide web for company . . .*

The secret garden is a flagstoned terrace surrounded by high walls built into a steep bank. Trees that were planted years and years ago trail their long arms down towards the surface of a pond. Dad told me that big golden fish called Japanese carp once lived there, but that they'd all been eaten by herons. To try and keep the real herons away, he'd got a fibreglass statue of one in Homebase and put it standing by the pond – a bit like a heron scarecrow – but it hadn't worked. The fake heron now stands in the glass porch that fronts the Gingerbread House. It had been 'made redundant', Dad told me.

That's what happened to Mama. She'd been 'made redundant' too. And that's why she is spending three weeks living here, to bring in some badly needed cash.

I was the one to christen it the Gingerbread House – years ago, when I was small. I guess most people thought it was a cute compliment because it looks like a cottage you'd see in an old-fashioned picture book: the kind of place that might house a little old lady – a sweet, plump, rosy-cheeked dame

2

with white hair in a bun who would welcome children into the garden when the fruit was ripe and red on the apple trees and invite them with a smile to help themselves.

But one day when we were driving home I heard Mama tell Dad that his mother had turned into a right witch. That was the real reason behind calling this place the Gingerbread House, because in the fairy tale that's where the witch lives.

I move to the pond. There are tadpoles in it – big fat ones wriggling about in the murky water – and snails sliming around the water's edge. As I sit down on the bench that catches the most sun, a picture-book illustration of another witch flashes before my mind's eye: a witch who lived in a house built from the bones of drowned sailors. Snails and sea slugs climbed along her fish tail and nestled in her matted hair, she was covered in scales and warts, and her chin boasted a small tuft of beard. This was the witch who cut out the Little Mermaid's tongue. We've that in common, the little mermaid and me – since I too have lost the power of speech.

I look down and notice that the wooden seat of the bench is rotting. Will Dad ever bother to replace it, I wonder? Or the mouldering blue plastic that lines the pond? Or the splintering trellis that clings to the wall in the patio garden below? The trellis flanks sliding glass doors that open on to the bedroom where the witch sleeps. I wonder if she's sleeping now, or did her carer get her out of bed today because Mama and Dad were coming?

The witch wasn't always a witch. Dad told me that years ago she had been a very beautiful woman: an actress who had played the lead role in *Jane Eyre* in a West End theatre production. I know about *Jane Eyre* because Mama and I went through a phase where we used to cuddle up on the sofa and watch DVDs together – historical dramas, mostly. I didn't enjoy all of them, but I watched them to keep Mama company, and I'm glad now that I did. Anyway, Dad said that some important film people saw the production of *Jane Eyre* that his mother was in – because lo! it is she who lives in this house – and asked her if she would like to go to a place called Pinewood Studios to do a screen test. But Granny got married instead to an important businessman who was very proud to take her as his wife because she was so beautiful and elegant.

I never knew my grandpa: he died before I was born. I suppose you could say that I never knew my granny either – the glamorous actress who existed before the witch took her over. The granny I know has a turned-down mouth and stony eyes that stare, even though she can't see much. The granny I know uses offensive language and shouts at people. The granny I know farts and picks her nose and coughs without putting her hand over her mouth.

I remember I came out here once with my friend Lola, and Granny farted, and Lola couldn't stop giggling, and I pretended to find it funny too but really I was mortified. Lola's granny is a Silver Vixen who goes travelling and does Pilates and wears flowery Doc Martens. Come to think of it, most of my other friends seem to have cool grannies, too. I am the only person I know who has a witch for a granny.

Dad told me that the witch started to take over when I was about four. Until then Granny had been living on her own in the pink-washed house. She had planted the clematis that grows around her front door and windows and had tended the plants in the glass porch. She had driven to the nearby village to post her letters (how quaint is that?) and to buy her supplies and pick up the daily paper. The paper was important because it kept her informed about what was going on in the world beyond this remote neck of the woods, as well as telling her what was on television. And the other good thing about it was the crossword. Dad told me that she used to do the crossword every day until her eyesight started to go and the holes began appearing in her brain.

To help me understand what had happened, Dad got a piece of Swiss cheese out of the fridge and showed me the holes in it. The cheese was like Granny's brain, and the more holes that appeared in it, the worse Granny's disease would become. The disease is called vascular dementia. So the reason that I had never really known my granny was because all those holes had started cropping up when I was very young. I had got to know the witch instead.

I hear the car boot slam, and I stand up and look over the wall. Below, Dad is pulling Mama's wheelie case into the house. All the supermarket carrier bags from the big shopping trip they did earlier have been unloaded onto the tarmac, and Mama is picking them up two at a time and taking them inside. There are a lot of bags. Three weeks is a long time to be living by yourself in a witch's house, and Mama has no transport, no way of buying fresh food.

When Mama got the word that she was being made redundant, we all three knew that she would never get another job. She worked in an advertising agency, and once you are a woman who hits forty in advertising you are too old. The only people they want in advertising any more are what Mama calls 'Young Turks'. So the three weeks we are spending here are a kind of trial period, to see if Mama might become Granny's carer while the usual carer, Lotus, takes time off. She's going home to Malaysia because her daughter is getting married.

Moneywise, things have got really bad: so bad that Mama cannot even afford to go to the hairdresser. We can't survive on what my dad brings in. He's a freelance journalist, and articles that used to take three days to write and bring in five hundred pounds still take three days to write and bring in two hundred pounds. He says the future of print journalism is that there's no future for print journalism. I know this, because I eavesdrop. Not in any spooky, nasty way, you understand, but simply because I can't help it. Our house is small, and you can hear everything.

Mama's finished carrying in the shopping and now she's taking her computer case out of the car boot. She is going to start writing a novel while she is here. I think she is being optimistic. I do not think that the witch's house is conducive to writing a novel.

Conducive. I love that word. I use big words a lot for one so young: English has always been my favourite subject at school. I guess it's because Mama used to read to me constantly until I could read for myself – she told me that she even read me stories while I was still in her tummy. And she taught me unusual words. I remember once going for a walk in some woods and Mama stopped and put her finger to her lips and said, 'Listen! What can you hear?' And I listened hard, but all I could hear was the wind rustling through the branches of the trees overhead.

'I hear the wind,' I told her.

She smiled and said, 'The sound you hear is called "soughing". That's what the wind is doing. It's *soughing* in the trees.'

I never forgot that. And I never forgot the stories she read me. They're all stacked inside my head.

I suppose my head is a kind of virtual library. I'm lucky

that way – I can take a story out any time I like and tell it to myself. Honestly, you could test me on anything. *The Little Mermaid*, for example. It begins: 'Far out in the wide sea, where the water is as blue as the loveliest cornflower, and where it is very, very deep, live the Mer-people.' And it ends like this: 'Unseen, our little mermaid leaped up and kissed the prince's forehead, then sped out of sight across the surface of the sea. And, for the first time in her life, her eyes were wet with tears.' That's when her heart breaks with sorrow, you see, and she's turned into foam on the waves. The Disney version has a happy ending, which I think is stupid.

Mama's eyes were always wet with tears when she finished reading me *The Little Mermaid*. She'd dash them away with the back of her hand – laughing and crying at the same time – and she'd say, 'Oh, it's so *sad*!'

And of course the stories that made her cry the most were the ones where the parent figure died – *Bambi* and *Charlotte's Web* and poor Aslan in *The Lion, The Witch and The Wardrobe*.

All this talk of crying must make you think that Mama's a real wuss! She's not. She laughs a lot – well, she used to – and she has a totally quirky sense of humour. She taught me how important it is to take the piss – especially when it comes to ads. Even though she worked as an advertising copywriter, she always sent the ads up rotten. For example, when I wanted her to buy Kitten Soft loo roll because of the picture on the front, she told me to think hard about it and make the connection. When I did, we both laughed out loud. Who would want to wipe their bum with a fluffy white kitten? And she was especially scathing about the shouty ads where people hector you to buy their product. Hector.

That's another good word she taught me.

The novel Mama's going to write is a thriller. She got loads of books out of the library so that she can do research while she's living out here, miles from anywhere. Apparently 'grip lit' is the new big thing in books. Dad joked that after three weeks of living with his mother she would have no shortage of material for a misery memoir. 'Gothic horror, more like,' she said. I've noticed that my parents' sense of humour has grown darker lately: I think it is what they call 'gallows humour'.

Mama says that book deals are the new lottery. It was in the news that an eight-year-old girl had signed a book deal. Who would want to read a book by an eight-year-old girl? I certainly wouldn't. An eight-year-old girl has no experience of life. I may be only fourteen, but even a fourteen-year-old could do better than somebody six years her junior. My life experiences include a red-carpet event, doing a voice-over for charity and scuba diving.

Both my parents are advanced scuba divers, and I learned to dive as soon as it was legal for me to do so, which was just after my tenth birthday. Mama said her heart was in her mouth when she saw me perform my first backward roll off the dive boat, so small and skinny I was, and weighed down with dive gear. But I took to it like a duck to water – ha ha.

We went on diving holidays to Malta and Jamaica after I certified, and I felt very proud to be a member of a mer-family. They were brilliant holidays – especially Jamaica. I finally knew exactly how it felt to *be* the little mermaid and live in that fantasy world below the sea. But Jamaica was the last holiday we had before Mama lost her job and the Young Turks took over.

Mama's in the porch: she's brought the last bag in. I'd

8

better go in too – I don't want to have to go through the patio doors to Granny's bedroom in case she's lying there in bed. She looks so scary – like a skull against the pillows – and when she takes her teeth out, her mouth is a gaping black hole.

In the porch, the redundant heron stands guard over a load of pots that have sad-looking witheredy-up plants in them. Maybe Mama will be able to resuscitate them: she has, as they say, green fingers. That's something else she could do to keep her occupied while she's stuck out here in the sticks: work in the garden.

I follow Mama into the sitting-room. It used to be quite a smart room, but it has a neglected air about it now. The covers on the armchairs are worn and grubby, and there are marks on the walls where paintings used to hang. Other paintings have been put up in their place, but they're the wrong shape, and they don't cover up the grey outlines left by the more valuable ones that had to be sold to pay for Granny's keep.

Other things have been sold as well. A pair of bronze lions. A porcelain dinner service, some furniture. Bits of jewellery that had real stones in them, not glass. I suppose the house will have to be sold some time, too, and Granny put into a home. But who would want to buy the Gingerbread House?

I look around with a critical eye. The sitting-room is bright and sunny because it has windows on three sides – a lick of paint is really all it needs, and new curtains.

But let me take you on a tour of the rest of the house, and you'll see what I mean.

2

LEO RISING

Come with me, outside into the hall. To our left is the sun
porch, so that means it's not too dark here. But take just two
or three steps along the corridor that leads past the study
and the kitchen and it's a different story. Whoosh! We are
plunged into gloom! It is as if we have been sucked into a
house designed by a vampire who could not tolerate light.
Mama made a joke about the study: she called it 'the Brown
Study', quoting an old saying that goes: 'Lack of company
will soon lead a man into a brown study.'

Being in 'a brown study' is a way of saying that you are
depressed, and yes – the study is all brown and dreary.
There's a pattern of brown autumn leaves on the loose
covers, and a muddy-coloured swirly pattern on the carpet,
and beige and brown wavy stripes on the curtains. The
study is where the television is, so Granny spends quite a lot
of time in here, watching David Attenborough DVDs, even
though she cannot see the screen properly. She just loves
the sound of David Attenborough's voice. She's sitting here
now, with her back to me. On the table next to her is a large-
print book, a glasses case and a magnifier. Granny doesn't

read any more, but she likes to pretend she can. She wears a wristwatch so that she can tell the time, but because she can't decipher the numerals, the time for Granny is always day or dark night or the dusky in-between.

The kitchen is further along the corridor, on the right. Louvred doors separate it from a breakfast room, but who would want to start the day by eating breakfast here? You'd have to turn the light on. The floor is made of cork tiles, and you sense that if you were to take your shoes off, the tiles would be sticky under your bare feet. In a corner of the ceiling there's a damp patch, and the wallpaper beneath has started to peel away.

Beyond the kitchen window is a bird table, but no birds visit now. Once Granny's eyesight started to go, she stopped putting out food for them because she couldn't see them properly. Dad says that Granny was a bit of a twitcher once – you know, a person who loves watching birds – and sure enough, there are loads of ancient bird books on the shelves in the Brown Study. The dodo is probably in some of them.

Out into the corridor we go. On the left is the pink bedroom; directly ahead is the door that leads into the garage. This door is always locked because burglars came through the garage into the house once when Granny was away. That was around the same time as the holes in her brain started happening, around the same time as she started doing things like leaving her handbag on the bench outside the front door and not showing up for appointments. That was when Dad knew she needed someone to come and live with her and look after her.

I hate that locked door. It has a fox's head hanging over it, stuck on a piece of wood shaped like a shield. The story is that Granny shot the fox years ago before she came to

11

live in the Gingerbread House. She shot it for humanitarian reasons, because it was lame, and she was so proud of her marksmanship that she had the head stuffed and mounted. Its glassy eyes stare down at me in a kind of accusing way: I always try not to look up.

The pink bedroom was pretty once, but like the rest of the house it's shabby now. The clematis I told you about grows around the window, and while this looks very charming and picture-postcardy on the outside, it blocks the light from entering the room. There are ornaments here that I remember playing with when I was little: a row of white china foals prance along the shelf above the bed.

This is where I will sleep with Mama tonight and for the rest of our stay here: the bed is just big enough for two. There's no way I'm sleeping in the blue room, which is where we are going next. It is poky and smells musty, and it's even darker than the breakfast room and the Brown Study. I really, really hate this room. It's where I had to sleep when I was small, and I remember once waking up in the middle of the night to see Granny looking down at me and reaching out a hand. I think she was probably trying to do something affectionate like stroke my hair, but I freaked and started screaming, and Granny teetered backwards like a startled gargoyle and fell out of the room. That was the last time we stayed over as a family. Now, when there's a changeover in the carers, poor Dad has to come out on his own and spend the night.

There are two carers. Well, there *were*. Lotus – who is here now – is lovely. She is from Malaysia, and she has a big smile. She must have been very young when she had the daughter who is getting married because she can't be much older than Mama, who is forty (admittedly, she has been forty for some years now). Dad is forty-eight, which means that Granny had him when she was over forty. Does that mean that Mama could have a baby, still? I wonder what it would be like to have a baby sister or brother. I like being an only child. Call me a loser, but I've always enjoyed being solitary. I suppose it's something to do with all the stories in my head that I take out and tell myself. I think that as long as your head is full of stories, you will never get lonely.

Granny was an only child too, and she *never* seems to be lonely. Not so long as she has David Attenborough DVDs or her audiobooks. She likes thrillers mostly. I remember one Christmas we stayed here and Dad got a new Agatha Christie audiobook for Granny as a present. It was called *Appointment with Death*, and when he put it in her CD player the first line that came out through the speakers was, 'You do see, don't you, that she's got to be killed!'

'What? *What? Who*'s got to be killed?' squawked Granny. 'Are they talking about me?' I remember Mama and Dad both clamped their hands over their mouths in an attempt to stop Granny from hearing their splutters of laughter. I told you they had a gallows sense of humour.

Let me take you into the bedroom now, where Granny sleeps. It's quite a big room, and because there are floor-to-ceiling glass doors opening out onto the patio garden you'd expect it to be full of light. But it faces the wrong way. If you were lucky, you might get some early morning sun dribbling into this room, but the curtains are always drawn until later in the day, when it's time for Granny to have her breakfast. By then, the sun has moved on. I wish the windows were open now: the room is stuffy, and there's that old lady smell of wee mixed with talcum powder.

Granny used to sleep in a double bed, but that's gone, and

she sleeps in a single bed now, like a child. There's a railing on one side in case she falls out, and a white vinyl backrest. Her bed always has lots of soft toys on it: there seem to be more every time I come here. There's a kitten and a puppy and a tiger, and several lions ranging in size from mini to real lion cub size because Granny's star sign is Leo. Leo, king of the jungle. Regal by name, regal by nature. I'm Pisces. A little fish.

I take a peek into Granny's wardrobe to see if the feather boa that Mama gave her for Christmas is still there. It is. Mama gave it to her because she thought it might be nice for Granny to wear something around her neck that would feel soft and silky to the touch, since touch is one of the five senses that Granny still has. But I've never seen Granny wear the boa. At the bottom of the wardrobe there is a row of shoes. They're dusty.

I hear voices in the corridor outside the room. Mama and Lotus are investigating the airing cupboard: Lotus is showing Mama where the switches are for the hot water. It's a long time since Mama was here last: she's probably forgotten how things operate. She's a bit of a klutz, my mum; anything technical is beyond her. It took Dad ages to teach her how to download and stuff. I'm amazed that she managed to pass her advanced scuba course: there are loads of techie things involved and Mama doesn't even know how to change a plug.

Granny likes Lotus. She didn't like the other carer, who was from Belfast. She was called Brid. Granny thought Brid was common, and she hated the sound of her voice. When Brid went out one day, Granny told her not to bother coming back, so Brid said 'Good riddance to bad rubbish' in her Belfast accent and handed in her notice. Lotus has a

14

lovely voice: it's bubbly and smooth at the same time, like an Aero bar.

'You won't need to switch the water to "bath",' Lotus is telling Mama, 'except for once a week, when you bathe her. I'll show you how to operate the electric chair in a minute.'

'The electric chair?'

Lotus laughs. 'The one in the bath that lowers her into the water. I call it her throne.'

'So a bath once a week is enough?'

'Sure. And a wash every day.'

'That'll be challenging.'

'But sometimes she tells me no wash, and I leave her alone because I do not want an argument. Arguments are a waste of energy. It's OK to leave her for one day without a wash, but no more, because then she will start to smell.'

'Oh, god. How do you do it?'

'I put her standing by the basin because that way she has something to hold on to. Her legs are wobbly, you know? I do her face with a flannel, and use a sponge for under her arms and between her legs. Front bottom first, then back. And sometimes I give her a toothbrush and ask her to do her teeth. She hates to clean her teeth, so anytime I see her dentures lying around, I grab them and give them a scrub.'

An intake of breath from Mama. A pause. Then, 'What about dressing her?'

'Keep it simple. There's no need to fuss around with buttons and zips – except if she's going out. I dress her today because it's special, with her family coming. But she finds dressing too exhausting, with all the bending and twisting. Most days I just put on a clean nightdress, and one of her long cardigans. She prefer a cardigan to a dressing gown. She says it is more elegant. And she always like to wear her wristwatch, even though she cannot see it well enough to tell the time. She finds it comforting.'

'Has she had any – um – accidents recently?'

'No. She is good, since that last urinary tract infection. But sometimes early in the morning she gets out of bed and does poo poo before I am awake, and I cannot wipe her.'

'You *wipe* her?'

Lotus shrugs. 'Sure. When I can. She cannot do it herself, see? I use baby wipes, and there are disposable gloves on the shelf above the loo.'

'Gross.'

'Yes. It is gross, but these things have to be done.'

'How often do you change her bed linen?'

'If things go good, once a week. But you must check every day to see if the sheets need changing. Here – see – I have a complete fresh set ready to go, in case of accident. And there are pants with pads in the top drawer of her chest-of-drawers, in case of emergency. In case the urinary tract infection comes back.'

'Can she wear them at night?'

Lotus laughs – a warm gurgle of a laugh. 'I have tried, but she just yell and throw them at me. She's not used to wearing panties in bed.'

'She *throws* them at you?'

'Sure, sure. She has a temper! And sometimes she uses bad language. She say things like "Fuck off, you fucking bitch – who do you think you are, ordering me about?" But I just say, "Don't talk to me like that, Eleanor. I'm just trying to take care of you. Don't you know how lucky you are to have a family who care so much about you that they make sure you are comfortable in your own home with someone to wash you and cook for you?"' Another laugh. 'And then

16

she say, "I'm perfectly capable of looking after myself, thank you. And I'll have you know I'm an excellent cook."'

Lotus mimics Granny very well.

'So she's abusive?'

'Sure. If she do not get her own way. She grab my arm if I'm on the phone, in how you call . . . a Chinese burn, yes? And take the phone from me. She gets jealous, see? She throw water at me when I try and get her in the bath – but you will be OK. You leave her bath till the weekends when Donn is here. You are lucky to have a strong man to help you.'

'Yes.'

The sound of Granny whistling comes from the Brown Study. It is not a tune she is whistling, it's the way you'd whistle for a dog.

'That is the worst thing. When she whistles for you.' Lotus's voice sounds a little tight.

'She's whistling for *you*?'

'Yes. But if you go once when she whistles, she will expect you to come again and again. I tell her, "I am not at your beck and call, Eleanor, OK? I am not your dog."'

'Dear god. I'd lose it if she whistled for me.'

'No, no. It is not good to get angry. Sometimes it's easy to get angry if you are tired, and then rows happen, and that is bad for both of you. I tell you again – arguments are a waste of time. It's important that you look after yourself, Tess, you understand? Eat properly, keep yourself healthy and strong, and take time out to rest and exercise.'

'I brought my yoga mat with me.'

'That's good. But you need fresh air, too.'

'So it's OK to leave her?'

'For thirty-five, forty minutes, sure. If she's been toileted and has something to watch on television.'

The whistle comes again, and Lotus ignores it. 'Stick to a regular routine because otherwise she gets unsettled. Breakfast, wash, lunch, afternoon tea, dinner, bed. I give her the Aricept before bedtime because it helps her sleep.'

'Aricept?'

'Her drug. It's on her bedside table. If she doesn't take it, her dementia symptoms will become worse.'

'Worse!' Mama gives a mirthless laugh.

'She fusses sometimes about little things that are of no consequence, so I just tell her she will be seeing a doctor soon. She saw a podiatrist last week about her bunion. That did not go so well.'

'What happened?'

'She kicked like a mule.'

Mama's face goes very still.

'I've left a list of numbers on the kitchen counter,' continues Lotus. 'Doctor, hairdresser and so forth, and I've written down her pet likes and dislikes. Food, television, all that jazz.'

'I brought some story books to read to her.'

'She'll love that.'

'Everything OK?' It's Dad's voice. Mama doesn't answer.

'You look nervous, Tess,' says Lotus. 'There's no need to be nervous. You'll do fine. Eleanor likes you. When I tell her today that Tess is coming to stay, she say "Oh, good! Tess is such a sweet person." You can handle her, no problem. Just remember to establish your routine and stick to it. It will make life easier for both of you. Now . . .' Lotus's tone changes, becomes brisk. 'I'd better go. I want to be on my way before the traffic builds up.'

'What time's your flight?' asks Dad.

'Eight thirty.'

I hear their footsteps recede along the corridor, then Lotus's voice again, buoyant and cheerful this time. 'Goodbye, Eleanor! See you in three weeks' time!' A minute later, there's the slam of a car door, the sound of an engine starting up. She's gone.

I leave Granny's bedroom and move into the bathroom. There is carpet on the floor that used to be pale pink but it is covered in stains now. I hate to think what might have made the stains. The 'throne' is made of white metal with a plastic mesh seat. I'd quite like to have a go on it, but the idea of Granny's bare bum on the seat puts me off. There are bars for her to cling on to when she's getting in and out, and one of those mats with rubber suckers that make a squelchy noise when you pull them away from the bottom of the bath. On the shelves there are bottles and tubes, some of them have instructions written on them: 'To rub onto back, legs, feet, etc.' Is Mama going to have to rub fragrant unguents onto Granny? I read about 'fragrant unguents' in *Tales from the Thousand and One Nights*, and for ages I thought that 'unguents' was pronounced 'un-goo-ents' until Mama put me right.

I see a flutter outside the bathroom window. A blue tit has landed on the old nesting box that Dad put up on the windowsill years ago. The bathroom window is quite high up in the wall: it's a long, narrow, horizontal window – double-glazed, like all the windows in the Gingerbread House. The blue tit does that twitchy, nervous thing with its head, looking around to check for enemies, and then it pops through the little hole into the nesting box. There must be eggs in there – or even baby birds! Climbing onto the loo seat, I stand on tiptoe. There's something happening in there, all right – I can just make out the shape of a beak gawping open. Yay! My very own blue tit nest! I feel like Michaela Strachan in *Springwatch*.

In the hall, I hear the front door open again. Dad must be heading off.

Bye, bye, blue tits! Out of the bathroom, along the corridor I go, to where it branches into an 'L' shape. There, at the other end, where the evening light is hitting the hall, Mama and Dad are standing, holding on to each other. 'Let's concentrate on the positive side of things,' Dad's saying. 'Just think of all the work you'll get done on your novel. And we'll get your laptop hooked up to Skype with Lottie and Zoë and Liam, so you can talk to anyone, anytime you feel like it, morning, noon or night.'

Mama nods. Lottie is her sister, who lives in Australia – I've only met her twice – and Zoë is Mama's best friend, who's moved to Chicago, and Liam is my godfather, who lives in Paris. I chose him to be my godfather when I was eight. Mama always allowed me to choose my godparents: we never had a formal ceremony in a church or anything like that because we're not religious. I was seven when I chose my godmother, who is called Marian. She took me out for the day to the movies and then for a hamburger in Nando's, and when I chose Liam he took me to the funfair. We went on some wicked rides, and I remember looking down and seeing Mama's upturned face, paper white with horror. She is so fearful for me: in Jamaica that time she had to stop going on dives with me because she couldn't enjoy them; she just spent the entire hour underwater looking for me and worrying about me. She said I was like Tinkerbell in *Peter Pan* – here, there and everywhere at the same time.

Dad takes a step back. 'I have to go, darling,' he says. 'I'm sorry. I'll phone you later.'

He turns and passes through the sun porch. Mama and

I follow him to the car, and he gets in and guns the engine. Then he's gone. Together we move to the gates and wave until he has passed under the tunnel of trees on the road beyond the Gingerbread House, then the car is out of sight.

Mama shuts the double gates – first one, then the other. The clanging sounds like prison doors being slammed shut, the way you hear on telly. She takes a deep breath, and sets her shoulders back.

'Well, sweetheart,' she says. 'It's just you and me now.'

You, me and the witch.

3

VETIVER AND VANILLA

Mama is very clever. She has persuaded Granny to go to bed by promising her that she'll read her a story once she gets there. Granny was mutinous at first, demanding that she be read a story where she was, sitting in her armchair like Jack in *Father Ted*. But Mama got round her in the end.

I wander down the corridor and listen by the door, but the story is a Roald Dahl one with a twist to the tale that I know already, so I don't stay to hear the end. Instead I wave goodnight to Granny and go back to the sitting-room, where Mama has set up her laptop. She told Granny that she would work in the sitting-room every day until the dot of six o'clock, then she would come into the Brown Study and bring Granny a nice G&T and they could watch the news together. I know for a fact that the G&T Mama will pour for Granny will be all T and no G. In order to make it smell like a proper drink, though, she will rub the rim of the glass with a little Gordon's gin. Dad's sister – my aunt, who sometimes has Granny to stay with her in her big house in Scotland – has told Mama that giving Granny alcohol is like taking a stick to beat yourself with. I suspect that Mama's G&T will contain *lots* of Gordon's.

There is an internet page displayed on the screen of Mama's laptop. Good. That means that broadband's connected: Mama was scared that it wouldn't work out here. I move closer to the screen and have a look. The file is called 'Caring for People with Dementia'. The page that is open lists tips for carers. The first one reads:

> Create a reliable daily routine with small rituals (from washing hands, saying prayers, preparing food, cleaning and singing to a little dancing before bedtime).

Prayers? Yikes. I don't imagine that Granny has said a prayer in her life. As for dancing before bedtime? Granny can hardly *walk*. And just what kind of dancing do these internet do-gooders have in mind? Old-time waltzes? The hokey-cokey? Or a *Strictly*-style cha-cha?

I resume my inspection of the web page. The next tip suggests:

> Obtain relief for yourself. People are not made to constantly carry such loads on their own.

In that case, I am very glad indeed that I am here for Mama. Somehow, between the pair of us, we'll get through.

I hear the sound of the television being turned on in the study. It's the BBC News theme tune. I don't like BBC News. I don't like watching any news programmes – I find them too disturbing. I'd much rather climb the stone steps to the secret garden and take out one of my stories and sit there with the evening sun on my face while I tell it to myself and listen to the blackbird's song.

But I don't want Mama to be in the Brown Study all on her own. So I go in and sit with her.

Mama is curled up in an armchair with her legs underneath her. She's refilled her glass. I pretend I don't notice.

I mosey over to the corkboard that hangs on the wall next to the window. Amongst the usual stuff like out-of-date special offers and flyers offering chimney-sweeping, roof repairs and so on, there are several newspaper cuttings – articles written by Dad with his byline photo. He looks much younger in his photo – smiling and tanned in an open-necked shirt, eyes half-obscured by a flop of hair. His hair is cut short now, to avoid committing the crime of a comb-over. There's an ancient picture of me standing beside a life-sized cardboard cut-out of Daniel Radcliffe, and next to that is a brochure for 'Elder Care Aids'. It features 'donut' ring cushions, long-reach toenail cutters, shower ponchos, lotion applicators and Bottom Buddies. Bottom Buddies? Oh, OK. Let's not go there.

The phone rings. Mama aims the remote at the telly to turn down the volume a notch or two. Then she picks up Granny's landline and presses 'answer'.

'Hey, Tess? Are you there?' Dad's voice comes across loud and clear on speakerphone, and I smile.

'Oh, Donn – thank Christ it's you. I thought it might be one of your mother's friends and I'd have to explain who I was.'

'My mother doesn't have any friends. They're all dead.'

'Shh! You're on speakerphone. I'll take you outside, in case Eleanor hears you.'

'Why don't you just turn speakerphone off?'

'I don't know how.'

'Just press the button on the —'

'No, no. I'm scared to press anything. I might get cut off.'

Mama unfurls herself from her armchair, picks up her glass and we leave the study. Yay! I'd much rather be outside. It's still sunny and the birds are going bonkers. I sit on the bench by the front door while Mama paces. She always paces when she talks on the phone.

'How are things?' asks Dad.

'Fab. Eleanor and I had a sparkling conversation over dinner about the weather. Graham Norton might have envied us our repartee.'

'Is she in bed now?'

'Yes.'

'How did you get her there?'

'I told her I'd read to her.'

'Good move. Tell me about it.'

Mama takes a hit of her drink. 'Well, it didn't seem too promising to begin with. At first she insisted that I read her a story there in the sitting-room, and I said no – I'd feel ridiculous reading a bedtime story to someone who wasn't in bed, and I said that if she didn't want a story I'd make myself useful by getting the dishes out of the way. So I went off and banged about in the kitchen, and next thing I hear her stomping down the corridor into her bedroom. So I go down, and say – all enthusiastic: "Oh, Eleanor! You've decided it's bedtime after all! That's great. I'll be able to read you a story now." And then I got her into her nightie and gave her her Aricept and read her the story. I had to skip some pages because it was way longer than I'd thought, but I don't think she noticed.'

'What did you read her?'

'That Roald Dahl one about the woman who murders her husband with the frozen leg of lamb. I realised too late that it wasn't the most uplifting choice. I think it left her feeling a little . . . nonplussed.'

'Is she settled now?'

'I hope so. I rubbed lavender balm on her temples and told her it would help her sleep. And then I kissed her goodnight and said "*Arrivederci*".'

'*Arrivederci*?'

'You once told me that "See you tomorrow" was the last thing she ever said to Maurice, and that she was superstitious about anyone saying it to her in case she'd wake up dead in the morning. So I said "*Arrivederci*" instead.'

'Try saying "See you tomorrow" next time and see what happens.'

They laugh a little wanly at this.

Maurice was my granddad. Heart disease got him in the end. He died in his sleep; they say that's not a bad way to go. I know that's what Dad hopes will happen to Granny – that she'll die in her sleep. He doesn't want her to fall, which is the way a lot of old people go in the end. They fall, and then they're carted off to hospital and they die in A&E on a trolley or in a public ward infested with MRSA. And while I know that Dad and Mama will be relieved when Granny finally dies, I also know that that is the last way they'd want her to pop off. Nobody deserves to die like that – not even the minister for health.

Granny did fall once. Lotus told Dad that she came across her lying on the floor of her bedroom, talking gibberish about some baby who was living in the wall of her bedroom. Granny said that she'd heard a baby crying, and when she'd gone to investigate, she'd seen its arm sticking out of the wall near the ceiling. I hope nothing like that happens while we are staying here.

But I don't think it's very likely that Granny will fall. She

26

is too cautious. The only time she moves from her chair is when she has to go to the loo – she calls it 'spending a penny' – and she walks so carefully that even if I accidentally brushed past her in the corridor, she would not be likely to topple over. It's funny, when she is sitting in her armchair she looks frail, as if she has sort of . . . sunk in on herself. But there is a scary kind of strength about her too. They say that animals caught in traps have a supernatural strength, and that's the kind I think Granny has.

'Oh – I nearly forgot,' says Mama, with a little laugh. 'She said a funny thing before I left the room. She said, "But you promised you'd read me a story!"'

'You mean she'd forgotten *already*?'

'Yep. There must be more holes than cheese in that brain of hers by now.'

'You're doing great, Tess. Carry on like this and you'll get through. Bedtimes will be no problem once you get some kind of routine going.'

'Yeah. Routine is key. That's what Lotus says, and that's what I keep telling myself.' Mama takes another hit of gin. 'The thing that scares me most is that she'll say something nasty and I'll let it get under my skin, and then we'll have a row. Lotus said that rowing's a complete waste of energy.'

'She's right. You've got to stay calm, no matter how much she provokes you. Remember how good you were at keeping your cool with the suits.'

The 'suits' were the clients that Mama's agency dreamed up advertisements for. The 'creatives' – like Mama – mostly despised the suits, but Mama used to feel sorry for them, stuck in those awful jobs like insurance and banking. She knew that when they brought their crappy ideas to the agency they were just like the deluded contestants on *Britain's Got*

Talent who believe they're headed for the Royal Variety. So she learned how to humour them and charm them, and as a result she usually ended up getting her own way.

'So far, I've been a positive amusement palace of pleasantness,' she says. 'I could apply for a job as a court jester.'

'There's an idea. Jokes.'

'What?'

There's a pause and the clackety clacking of computer keys and then Dad says, 'I'm looking at jokes online. Here's a good one.'

'Bring it on.'

'An old man goes to his doctor. The doctor tells the old man he has bad news, and he has extremely bad news. The old man asks for the extremely bad news first. "The extremely bad news is that you have cancer," says the doctor. "Oh. That *is* extremely bad news," says the old man. "But now we've got the extremely bad news out of the way – what is the other news?" "The other news is that you have dementia." The old man thinks about this for a moment or two, and then he says, "Oh, well, I suppose things could be worse. I could have cancer."'

Mama laughs her tired laugh. 'Thanks for that, love,' she says. As she drains her glass, the ice cubes tinkle.

'Are those ice cubes?'

'Yes. I'm having a G&T. A large one.'

'You've earned it. You'll sleep well tonight.'

'Damn right.' She looks up at the sky, which is tinged with pink. 'The forecast is good. I'll be able to go for a run in the morning, once I've given Eleanor her breakfast.'

There's another pause, then Dad says, 'Here's another one. An old man and woman are talking in an old folks' home. The man says, "I'm so old I forgot how old I am." The woman says, "I'll tell you how old you are. Take off your clothes and bend over." The man does as she tells him, and the woman says, "You're eighty-four." The man is astonished, and says: "That's amazing! How can you tell?" The woman replies: "You told me yesterday."'

Mama laughs again and this time her laugh is the one I remember from the old days, exuberant and infectious.

'I'd better go, love,' says Dad. 'I've a deadline to meet.'

'Goodnight, Donn. I love you.'

'I love you, too. Goodnight, Tess.'

There's a click, and the line goes dead.

Mama looks up at the sky again. The sun has not yet dipped below the trees. 'I think I'll stay out here and read for a while,' she says, and I'm glad that we're not going back into the Brown Study to watch the news. A little girl has gone missing, and every day her parents look thinner and more and more wasted with worry. I think it must be easier for parents to know that their child is dead than to have to live on not knowing if they will ever see her again.

Mama goes into the house to fetch her book, and I watch a butterfly flutter in and out of the clematis. It reminds me of the fairy brasslets I used to see fluttering around the reefs in Jamaica. I loved the names of the fish, and can recite them still, like a mantra. *Shy hamlets, indigo hamlets, butter hamlets, flame fish, cardinal fish, trumpet fish, parrotfish, cherub fish, angelfish* . . .

'Wow! Get a load of this!'

I hear Mama's voice as she comes through the door. She's back with her book – except it isn't a book, it's an old-fashioned photograph album.

She sits down beside me and opens it randomly. I see a big

studio-type photograph of a beautiful young woman being clutched to the chest of a patrician-looking man. 'It's Granny as Jane Eyre,' murmurs Mama. 'How extraordinary.'

This beauty is Granny! It *is* extraordinary. Granny's unlined face is a perfect heart shape, her mouth is curved in a demure cupid's bow, her eyes are luminous below sleekly groomed brows, her glossy hair is held back with a simple ribbon. The bone structure of her face is exquisite: it bears no relation to the parchment-covered skull I see lolling on her pillow any time I pass her open bedroom door. She really could have been a film star.

Mama turns the page. There are more photographs – snapshots this time – of Granny playing golf, Granny in a swimsuit, Granny with her parents – linking their arms and smiling to the camera. As Mama turns page after page I see more images of a vibrant young woman, the picture of – how do they say it? – 'rude good health'. Here's Granny in tennis whites, brandishing a racket; here's Granny on holiday, larking on a beach; here's Granny holding a newborn. Dad as a baby? Mama confirms it. 'Donn,' she says, turning the last page.

Stuffed into the back of the album is an envelope. Mama opens it and empties out a wad of newspaper cuttings. They're all about Granny.

'Eleanor Sinclair,' I read, 'who is currently appearing in the Phoenix Theatre's acclaimed revival of Noël Coward's *Blithe Spirit*, was seen taking tea in the Savoy Hotel last Saturday. Miss Sinclair was the personification of elegance in a dove-grey tailored costume.'

Wow! So Granny even made it into the social columns! I suppose this is the olden days equivalent of the 'Spotted!' section in *Heat* magazine.

A shadow falls across the page. The sun has gone down below the trees. Mama gives a little shiver. 'Time to go inside,' she says, sliding the cuttings back into their envelope and shutting the album. 'Back to the joys of the Brown Study.' She picks up her empty glass. 'And a large nightcap, I think.'

She stands up and stretches, and then she moves into the sun porch, sliding the glass door to behind us. She flicks up the bolt, then reaches into her pocket, produces a bunch of keys and locks it with a Yale, testing to make sure it's secure. The front door, next. Once inside, she turns a stout key in the mortise, and we're well and truly locked in. She drops the keys into a raffia basket that sits on the table by the door and then she goes into the kitchen. I hear the sound of ice cubes being dropped into a glass.

I think I'll head to bed and tell myself a story.

In the pink bedroom, my teddy is tucked in under the flowery duvet. It's funny how people cling on to things like teddies, even when they're far too old for them. Dad told me it was nothing to be ashamed of: even Granny still had her teddy – until one of her dogs dispatched it shortly after she moved into the Gingerbread House.

Granny always had dogs. Mama says she hated them because once the dementia started creeping into Granny's brain she never washed them and they stank. I have a long-ago memory of Mama and I coming out here one day to bring Granny a bunch of Mother's Day flowers and the dog that was living here crapped on the cork-tiled floor of the breakfast room. I remember Mama picking the dog poo up with a plastic bag and nearly vomiting as she sped to the loo to flush it away.

Mama is quite squeamish. I wonder how she'll cope when

she has to wash Granny. Well, we'll find out tomorrow.

I close my eyes and start to drift away. When I was small, Mama told me that if I went to sleep at exactly the right time, the Dream Spinner would come and weave the best dreams for me, where I could go anywhere in the universe I wanted, with any companion I chose – Peter Pan or Nemo or Woody. I always chose Teddy.

The scent of my teddy is comforting. He smells of vetiver and vanilla. They are the base notes of Mama's perfume, she told me once. My teddy smells of Chanel No. 5.

4

A House Elf

The carriage clock by the bed says twenty to nine. Beside me, Mama's still asleep. She came to bed quite late last night, smelling of toothpaste and her new night cream. She used to always use Lancôme, but she's had to stop buying it because it's too expensive. I used to love it when they had promotions on and she'd bring back gift bags and let me have the freebies. Not that I'm really into make-up, but my friend Lola and I sometimes used to practise on each other. Lola's so pretty she could be a model. She has the longest eyelashes of anyone I know; when I used to put her mascara on, her lashes looked fake, they were so long.

Lola could never be a scuba diver – she's too vain. After my first training session in the pool, when I took my mask off, my face looked like the muzzle of some badly drawn cartoon character, and there was snot all round my nose. It's called 'diver's face' – it's got to do with pressure on the sinuses underwater. Some people think that scuba diving is a glamorous sport, but it's not. Other people think it's a macho sport, but it's not that either. How to describe it? It's serene, like what it must be like to be in heaven, if such a place exists. Jacques Cousteau – who was one of the first divers to use scuba – got it right. He said that underwater, man becomes an archangel.

More than anything, I would love to be able to free dive: that's when you go down with no bulky kit – no tank or BCD or regulator. It's just you and your weight belt and super-long fins, totally streamlined. In Jamaica, our dive instructor's son came on a dive with us once. He was a champion free diver – he could stay down for over six minutes. I'm not kidding! It was the most magical thing in the world to see him swim alongside us, untrammelled by gear, sleek as a seal or a dolphin – a proper mer-person! And then he'd swoop away, and you'd look up and see him hovering overhead – an angel without wings watching over you.

From outside the window, I hear the shrill tck tck tck alarm call of a wren. I wonder how my blue tits are getting on. I slide out of bed and move down the corridor towards the bathroom. I have to pass Granny's open door – she hates to sleep with it closed – and I wonder if she's awake or asleep. The curtains are still drawn, so I can't see too well, but I finally decide her eyes are closed. That doesn't necessarily mean she's sleeping, though. Lotus says she spends most of the morning in bed, just lying there with her eyes closed. I suppose she might be remembering what it was like to be young and beautiful and surrounded by beaux.

Lotus wrote down instructions for Mama, to do with Granny's routine, and stuck them on the fridge door with a magnet that says: *You don't have to be mad to work here, but it helps*. Lotus's routine goes like this: she brings Granny a bowl of Crunchy Nut Cornflakes at around nine o'clock, and some tea and toast at ten. Then she leaves her to it until it's time for her wash, just before lunch. After lunch,

Granny either 'watches' telly, or listens to one of her crime story CDs. Then a cup of tea and a pancake or a biscuit around four. Then supper. Lotus said that the routine is really, really important because if it gets disrupted, so does Granny, and then all hell breaks loose. Bedtime is the last thing on the list. Lotus doesn't read Granny a story: that was Mama's idea. I think Mama might even enjoy that bit of her routine: it might remind her of how she used to read to me when I was a baby.

Lola had a baby brother. She told me that it must be dead boring being a baby, because all they do is eat and sleep and poo. But I disagree. When you are a baby, you're learning all the time. I read somewhere that you learn more in your first year than in all the other years of your life put together, which means that being a baby must be way preferable to being a demented person who can learn nothing new. And when you think about it, all Granny does is eat, sleep and poo. Everything else is done for her.

What must it be like to be waited on hand and foot? Granny's always had staff. Mama told me that a woman called Prudence used to come in every day to do her housework until the dementia started to kick in big-time, and then Prudence resigned from the job. Granny had become so overbearing that even Prudence, who was her devoted servant (I imagine her as being a bit like Dobby in *Harry Potter*), could no longer stick being treated like a house elf.

I stop looking at Granny and go on into the bathroom to see how my blue tits are coming along. There is a turd floating in the loo.

There doesn't seem to be anything much happening in the nesting box beyond the window, but there, in the middle of the patio, are two white peacocks! Where did they come from? Is this a mirage? No, no mirage: they're real, moving around regally, as if they own the joint. I'm going to check them out from the comfort of the sitting-room, where I can watch them through the glass door that opens onto the patio instead of poking my head over the bathroom windowsill.

They make a funny noise, peacocks. It's spooky – a bit like a baby crying. As I watch them grubbing around between cracks in the crazy paving for worms, I hear sounds coming through the serving hatch that opens into the kitchen. Mama must be getting Granny's breakfast.

She is. I blow her a kiss, and she smiles.

Mama has sliced strawberries to put on top of Granny's Crunchy Nut Cornflakes. It's the end of the packet, and she's emptying the flakes into a bowl with a picture of a robin on it. Something tells me it's a bad idea to give Granny Crunchy Nut Cornflakes dregs, but I know my mother hates to waste anything. She adds the strawberries, and then a little cream, and then I see her take a deep breath as she steels herself for the wake-up call.

'Good morning, Eleanor!' she says, breezing into Granny's bedroom and setting the bowl down on the table. It's one of those tables that have 'L' shaped legs, so that you can slide them in under the bed. Mama does this, and then she moves to the window and pulls back the curtains. 'It's a beautiful day! The weather forecast was right, for a change!'

'Who's that?'

'It's Tess, Eleanor. I'm looking after you while Lotus is away. She's gone to Malaysia because her daughter's getting married.'

'Oh, yes.'

'Shall I hoosh you up?'

'I can hoosh myself up.' Granny makes an ineffectual

hooshing movement, and Mama takes advantage of this to slide another pillow behind her back. Granny's lolling over the tabletop now, reaching for something. Her teeth. She slides them in, and then picks up her spoon and starts to eat the cornflakes. I knew Mama should have opened a fresh packet. Granny's expression changes from one of resigned routine to one of thunderous outrage. 'They taste of dust!' she fumes. '*Dust!*'

I almost expect her to add: 'Dust – I tell you! Dust!' but she doesn't. She just throws the spoon across the room. Mama bends down and picks it up, and I see her flinch, as if she's half-expecting Granny to hurl the bowl after the spoon.

'*Dust!*' says Granny again.

'Oh, dear,' says Mama, with remarkable *sangfroid*. 'I'd better fetch you a fresh bowl, then, hadn't I?' She picks up the bowl of Crunchy Nut Cornflakes and leaves the room. Her back is very rigid.

Sangfroid means 'cool' – the literal translation is 'cold blood'. I suspect that Mama's going to need intravenous anti-freeze if she's going to get through the next twenty days. I will her not to lose her temper, I will her to stay strong.

Granny lies back against the pillows, looking as if she's wearing a death mask. 'Dust,' she says again. 'This room is dusty.'

Actually, it isn't. Lotus obviously did a big cleaning job before she got sprung.

'And it's very messy,' continues Granny. 'Why are your clothes strewn all over the place?'

For a moment I wonder if she's talking to me, but she's given no indication that she's seen me. And there are no clothes strewn over the bedroom floor. What's she talking about?

'Well, Maurice?' says Granny, in a peremptory voice. 'Do you expect me to pick up after you? I must say that I have no intention of doing so. I did not marry you to be your servant, and if you think I did, then you have another think coming. You must put your own clothes away. What? I *beg* your pardon? Then we are clearly going to have a row. My mother told me that I must never tidy up anyone's mess other than my own. You make your bed, you must lie in it. I am going to report you to her. I am going to pick up the phone to Mother right now and tell her to come over here. I might even get into the car and drive myself to her house. Yes. That is exactly what I am going to do. I am going to drive to Mother's. And when I come back, I want every trace of your clothing hung back in the wardrobe. Is that loud and clear?'

Mama is standing in the doorway, holding a fresh bowl of Crunchy Nut Cornflakes. She is looking at Granny with an expression that is half-apprehensive, half-fascinated. She takes a step into the room, and Granny says: 'Who is it?'

'It's Tess, Eleanor, with a fresh bowl of Crunchy Nut Cornflakes for you.' Mama sets the bowl on the bedside table, then takes a step backwards. 'Would you like to listen to the radio?' she asks. She switches on the old-fashioned transistor by the bed and didgeridoo music floats out. It's spookily lovely, but Granny clearly doesn't think so.

'You call *that* listening to the radio?' she says scathingly. Mama bites back a remark and flicks the off switch. Then she leaves the room without a backward glance and goes into the kitchen. I go with her.

'She was talking to Maurice. Oh, help me, Katia. She was talking to her dead husband. Oh – where's the phone, where's the phone, where's the phone?'

It's on its recharger, in the hatch between kitchen and sitting-room. But there's something else there, too. It's a spider. It's the biggest, blackest spider I've ever seen, and Mama's seen it too.

'Oh, crap, oh, crap. Oh – how do I get rid of it?' she says in a panicky voice.

Mama never kills spiders. The first time she read *Charlotte's Web* to me I made her vow that she would never kill one, ever. We even have a device on a stick at home that allows you to capture insects like spiders and bumble bees at a remove, so that you can set them free in the garden. But this is like a CGI spider from a horror film that would eat Charlotte as a snack. I nod solemnly, granting Mama permission to exterminate. Her breathing is ragged as she rummages in the cupboard beneath the sink. She emerges with a can of fly spray.

'Oh god oh god oh god.'

Wresting off the cap, Mama stretches out an arm, aims the can at the spider, pushes down on the nozzle – and suddenly the creature is covered in toxic white foam. It goes into a spasm, springs to the rear of the hatch, shudders once or twice . . . and then goes still.

Mama sets down the fly spray, then leans up against the louvred doors that separate the kitchen from the breakfast room. Her breathing is rapid and shallow: if you saw her in a film you might think that she has just committed a murder. Which she has, in a way. I don't think she's killed anything in her life, apart from flies. And the other thing is that she knows it is very bad luck to kill a spider. Mama allows herself time to calm down, and once her breathing's got back to normal, she reaches for the phone.

No! It lives! The bugger makes a kind of bouncy movement

and Mama shrieks and lunges for the fly spray with her free hand, dousing the insect as if it's on fire and she's trying to put it out. The spider goes apeshit – like an ink doodle in motion – and then it falls over the edge of the hatch into the recycling bin.

'Oh god oh god oh god.'

Mama hits autodial as she speeds through the breakfast room, heading for the front door. Dad picks up on the third ring. By now she's out in the garden and speakerphone is in competition with birdsong.

'Hi. It's Tess calling from the house of horrors,' she says.

'What's happened?'

'The Crunchy Nut Cornflakes tasted of dust. She tried to brain me with a spoon. She's giving out yards to your dead father for not hanging his clothes back in the wardrobe. She's threatening to drive to her mother's house. And I've just had a close encounter with an arachnid that even her beloved David Attenborough would find repellent.'

'So it's a case of business as usual, yes?'

'I guess you could say that.'

'How are things in the hygiene department?'

'What do you mean?'

'Has she been to the loo?'

'Definitely.'

'OK.' Dad gives a sigh. He's thinking. He always sighs when he's thinking hard. 'Leave her alone for an hour. Plug yourself into your iPod and get out your yoga mat.'

Mama does yoga every morning: she's very, very bendy. When Mama told Dad that bendy people tend to live longer, he laughed and said in that case Granny was the exception that proved the rule. I don't think Granny ever took any form of exercise after she hit middle age. Not even in the form of housework, since she had Dobby to do it for her.

'There's no way I'm plugging myself into my iPod while I'm living in this house,' says Mama.

'But you love your iPod.'

'I know. But I'll need to keep my wits about me in case your mother sneaks up and starts firing missiles at me. I'll head out for a run after I've brought her some tea and toast.' Mama shoots a glance at her watch. It's a Patek Philippe that Dad got her one Christmas before the Young Turks came to power. 'I'll go and do that now – she'll have finished her cornflakes.'

'Wait. I've a good one for you.'

Mama smiles. 'Bring it.'

'An old man hobbles up to an ice-cream van and orders a cone. "Crushed nuts, granddad?" asks the ice-cream man. "No," replies the old man. "Rheumatism."'

'Bye, Donn!' Mama switches off the phone with a laugh, just as a white peacock rounds the corner of the Gingerbread House. 'Look, Katia! A white peacock! Are they supposed to be lucky, or unlucky?'

I shrug. Lola's mum once told me that keeping peacock feathers in the house was bad luck, but I don't know about peacocks outside. I suppose people wouldn't keep them if they were unlucky.

Mama goes back into the house. 'Time for tea, said Zebedee,' she says.

41

5

A Waste Of Fairy Dust

Mama's plugged herself into her iPod and gone off for a run.
From the garden down the road I hear the peacocks shriek
as she passes.

I compiled a playlist for her ages ago to encourage her to
download more music, but she wasn't interested: she doesn't
seem to mind listening to the same old stuff. As I watch her
set off up the road, I wonder what she's listening to. I like
to think it's mento, the music played by The Jolly Boys,
the band who used to play every evening at the resort we
stayed at in Jamaica. How I would have loved to have had a
waterproof MP3 player on that holiday: imagine being able
to listen to music during a dive!

I'm up by the pond, watching damselflies dart over the
stagnant surface of the water. I wonder where Mama will
go on her run. To the foot of the mountain, probably. I'd
say it's beautiful up there at this time of year, with the gorse
blazing yellow and bluebells carpeting the woods. We used
to follow rabbit trails along the slopes there when I was little
and make up stories about who lived in the burrows.

Once upon a time, we drove out here every other week to

climb the mountain or go wandering in the woods. And then Mama got spooked by a man creeping around in the bushes with his thing hanging out, and we started going to the local National Trust gardens instead so that we could ramble without running the risk of bumping into pervs. Mama reasoned that you don't run into many pervs on National Trust property. Sometimes Lola would come with us and we'd pretend that we lived in the Big House and that the grounds belonged to us. I miss Lola. I wonder how she is, now she's living in New York: we kept in touch by e-mail for a while after she moved, but we've drifted apart.

Thinking about Lola makes me feel lonely, suddenly. It's time to take out a story. Which one? There are dozens and dozens to choose from, and Disney's done them all. *Snow White, Pinocchio, Cinderella, Alice in Wonderland, Sleeping Beauty, Peter Pan* . . .

Peter Pan was another of the stories that used to make Mama cry – the end bit when Peter comes back and wants Wendy to fly off with him again to Neverland. But by then Wendy has grown up and has a daughter of her own, and she doesn't know how to fly any more. In Neverland, only the light-hearted and innocent can fly. In Neverland, you don't waste fairy dust on olds. I settle down on the weathered bench and begin to tell myself the story: 'All children, except one, grow up . . .'

*

Mama's back: I can hear the sound of the gate opening. I guess she'll have a shower now and then settle down to work on her novel.

I move down to the patio: the sun has left the secret garden and climbed westward. That's the one good thing about

43

the Gingerbread House: while the sun rarely penetrates its interior, outside you can follow its orbit all day long. It shines first on the secret garden, then the patio, then the lawn, and finally on the front of the house, where Mama and I sat on the bench last evening, looking at Granny's photograph album.

The swing seat on the patio has a direct view of Granny's bedroom through the sliding doors: I can see that she's eaten the toast that Mama brought her earlier and is lying back against the pillows again. She's taken her teeth out, and her mouth is gaping open. The swing seat creaks. Granny turns her head and says, 'Is that you, Katia?' Maybe she remembers sitting there with me when I was a baby: there is a framed photograph of us on the wall of the Brown Study, Granny under the canopy looking chic in a crisp white shirt, me looking gormless in a bib and bonnet. Beyond the bedroom door I catch a glimpse of Mama in the corridor, heading for the bathroom wrapped in a towel.

From a neighbouring garden, one of the peacocks calls. I close my eyes. It's pleasant to sit here, on the swing seat with the sun on my face. Maybe Granny doesn't have such a bad life after all, lying there with her memories as bedfellows. I have loads of happy memories to keep me company, too. We are an almost sickeningly happy family, even 'in times of adversity', like now. I sometimes feel dysfunctional because I am so 'wholesome', as Lola put it. So many of the books in the Young Adult section of the library centre on teen suicide and bullying and eating disorders, and most of my friends have problems with their parents or step-parents or other members of their big extended families. I found myself pretending that I too suffered bouts of neurosis and low self-esteem so that I wouldn't stick out so much as a freak. But I drew the line at cutting myself, like some girls did, just to fit in.

44

I think Mama half-expected that the happy times might end when I hit puberty. She'd heard horror stories from other mothers about pubescent girls awash with hormones and hatred for their parents, but my puberty was pretty uneventful. Maybe it's because there was no sibling rivalry to contend with. Lola detests her older sister, and her older sister detests her right back.

Fishing around for memories, I hit on some special ones. The day we went swimming in a lake in Scotland and a gang of goats ate Dad's chinos; the day we dropped down into the shallows of the Blue Lagoon in Jamaica and took off our fins so that we could 'moonwalk' on the sandy bottom; the day we went to London for the premiere of the last *Harry Potter* movie . . .

My dad had got tickets because he was covering the event for a newspaper, and the cool girls in my year shrugged and went all 'whatever' when I told them I was going. So when I got back afterwards I didn't like to talk about it too much in case it sounded like I was boasting. But it *was* special. Not many girls my age have been to a red-carpet event. I've been lucky.

I remember how beautiful J.K. Rowling looked as she glided past in her rose-patterned dress, and the laugh that Hermione gave as she reached for Ron's hand and ran towards the dance floor; and the steam floating up from the gigantic caldron and the swish-swash of the chocolate fountain and the dazzling colours of the sweet stall and the smell of the hog roast that came drifting in from the balcony overlooking the Thames . . .

The sound of the glass doors sliding back makes me open my eyes.

6

THE SEA WITCH

An hour must have passed – maybe two. Mama has showered and dressed. She's wearing her blue linen shift dress. She has a blue and white silk scarf wound around her head, which means she's been working. She always ties a scarf around her head when she sits in front of her laptop, to keep her hair back from her face. It's got so long now – she used to have it cut gamine style in an expensive hair salon, but now she just twists it up in a knot or wears it in a plait.

'Who's that?' It's Granny's voice.

'It's Tess, Eleanor. I'm looking after you while Lotus is away. She's gone to Malaysia because her daughter's getting married.'

'Oh, yes.'

'I thought you might like to have a wash before lunch.'

'What? What are you talking about?'

'Well, I've run some water into the basin, and put on the heater in the bathroom, so it's nice and warm for you in there. And after we've had a wash, you might like to go into the sitting-room. There's a present waiting for you in there.'

'Who's it from?'

'It's from me.'

'Oh! How kind! Who did you say you are again?'

'I'm Tess, Eleanor.'

'Tess? *Tess?* Did you marry someone I know?'

'Yes, Eleanor. I married Donn.'

'You married Donn? My son, Donn?'

'Yes.'

'You don't mean to tell me that you two are married?'

'We are.'

'Why did nobody ever tell me? That's great news! I'm so happy to hear that! Welcome to our family, Tess!'

'Thank you. Would you like me to help you out of bed, Eleanor?'

'Why do I have to get out of bed?'

'We're going to have a wash, before lunch. And I'm going to look out a fresh nightdress for you.' Mama moves to the chest-of-drawers and takes out a nightdress. It's brushed cotton with a lace-trimmed collar and elbow-length sleeves. 'Let's see – this one's pretty. You're wearing a white one, so let's ring the changes and wear blue today.'

Mama's trying very hard to sound bright and upbeat, but I can hear the strain in her voice. I know she's dreading what's coming next.

'What's that you've got wrapped around your head?' enquires Granny.

'It's a scarf, Eleanor.'

'Aha! Fancy yourself, do you?'

'No, I don't fancy myself. It's to keep my hair back from my face. Now . . .' Mama pulls back the duvet cover. 'If you take hold of my hands, I'll help you up.'

Granny reaches out and grasps Mama's outstretched hands. 'Oh! Your hands are like stones!' she cries.

'No worries. It's lovely and warm in the bathroom.'

Granny's on her feet, teetering a little. 'Which way do I go now?' she asks.

'Out the door, to the left. Follow me.'

Mama leads the way into the bathroom. I follow Granny, who clutches onto the chest-of-drawers as she lurches past.

It's warm in the bathroom. Mama has turned on the electric heater that hangs high up on the wall. She's standing by the basin, testing the temperature of the water. 'Hmm. Yes, I think that's about right.'

'What do you want me to do now?' asks Granny.

'If you stand here, and hold on to the basin, I'll give your face a wash.'

'There are bubbles in there. I don't like soap.'

'It's not soap,' improvises Mama. 'It's an emollient.'

'A what?'

'A kind of moisturiser.'

Mama dips a flannel into the water, wrings it out, then proceeds to wipe Granny's face. Granny has her eyes squeezed shut, and her expression is that of someone doing penance. 'There's a thing,' she says, 'on my face.' Raising a bony hand, she points at an inch-long growth sprouting on the corner of her jaw.

'Yes, I know. No worries about that. Lotus has made an appointment for you with the doctor. She's going to take you to see him when she gets back from Malaysia.'

'And there's another one, here.' Granny points at a similar thing on her forehead. She's been picking at it, and it has formed a scab.

'The doctor will have a look at that too,' Mama tells her. 'You must try not to fiddle with it, Eleanor.'

'I don't *like* it!'

48

'No, of course you don't. But the doctor will take care of it.' Mama dips the flannel in the water, squeezes it, then assays another gentle swipe at Granny's face.

'That's enough!' says Granny.

'Fair enough. I'll get a towel.'

Mama reaches for a bath towel and hands it to Granny.

'It's heavy!'

'All right. I'll dry your face for you.' She does so, then drapes the towel over a rail. 'Now . . .' She's steeling herself. 'Arms up, and I'll help you off with your nightgown.'

For an awful moment, I think Granny is going to refuse to cooperate. But then she raises her arms, and Mama draws the gown over her head.

You don't want to know what the naked body of a ninety-year-old woman looks like. You really, really don't. But I'm going to tell you anyway, because you are going to have to get used to it. They say that pretty soon most people in the western hemisphere are going to live to be over a hundred, and all the beauty products in the world won't hold back the ageing process – in spite of what the likes of Sandra Bullock and Ellen DeGeneres are paid millions to say. So if you are squeamish, like Mama, I suggest you skip the next two paragraphs.

Granny's skin is as thin and transparent as cling film, apart from the skin on her bum. Her bum is leathery, and it's a mottled purplish colour. It reminds me of a miniature version of an elephant's bum on David Attenborough. Her tummy is like a deflated balloon, her boobs sag like empty silk purses, and the folds of her fanny droop like some exotic dead flower.

Her body is covered in liver spots and scales and growths, like you'd see on a whale shark. Some of the growths look like pebbles, and some of them look like snails – quite big ones. She's the sea witch in *The Little Mermaid*, and she smells of poo.

I'm sorry. That's the warts and all description over with. Now you know what most people don't.

'Raise your arm for me, Eleanor, will you please?' Mama takes a sponge and wipes first under Granny's left arm, then the right. She wipes the folds under the left breast, then the right. Then she gets to her knees. 'Can you part your legs for me?' she asks.

'It's a long time since anyone's asked me to do that!' quips Granny, and Mama manages to laugh obligingly.

She does as Lotus told her to: first front bottom, then back. But when she wipes the back, shit comes away on the sponge. I see Mama try not to gag. 'Hmm,' she says, hastily dropping the sponge back into the basin. 'I think we're going to need baby wipes for this job.'

'Baby wipes! I'm not a baby!'

'I know that, Eleanor, but there's poo coming away on the sponge, and it's really unhygienic.'

'Oh – you're such a fusspot! Little Miss Finickity Boots!'

'Bear with me.' Mama reaches for the baby wipes on the shelf. The first three she uses all come away with smears on. The fourth one comes away clean. 'You're very good, Eleanor. Very patient. I know it can't be easy.'

'Can I sit down now?'

'Yes. Let me just put a towel on there for you, to make it more comfortable.'

Mama lays a towel across the seat of a blue painted bentwood chair and Granny sits down with an 'Oof!' She really does look exhausted. She's been standing for maybe all of four minutes.

'How about a little talcum powder, to help dry under your arms?' Mama reaches for a tub of baby powder and sprinkles some onto her palms. Granny obediently raises her arms and allows Mama to anoint her with the talc before drooping again. 'And now let's get you into your nice clean nightgown. Here we go.'

Mama manages to get the collar of the blue gown over Granny's head, but the sleeves are problematic. Sliding her hand inside a cuff, she invites Granny to take hold of it. That way she can draw first one arm through, then the other.

Oh, yay, Mama! You've done it! You're nearly there!

Mama kneels again and guides Granny's feet into a pair of slippers. Granny's feet are like misshapen claws. The tendons look like ropes, and the bones jut out so far they look as if they might break through the skin. There is a massive bunion on the right foot.

'My foot hurts,' says Granny.

'I'll mention that to Lotus. She can ask the doctor to have a look at it when she takes you to see him.'

'And I have an itch.'

'Yes. I noticed that you've been scratching yourself.'

There were red score marks on Granny's thigh. I suppose the skin is so thin that any scratching damages it now. Mama told me once that in Granny's day nobody bothered with protection when they sunbathed. They just slathered themselves in oil and lay there soaking up the rays, roasting themselves. So all those growths on Granny's body must have been caused by sun damage.

'Now,' says Mama, all businesslike, 'shall I do your hair for you, or can you do it yourself?'

'I'll do it myself.'

'OK.'

Mama hands Granny a wide-toothed comb and she rakes it through her hair. She's a little thin on top, and there are flaky patches on the bald bit. When she's finished, she hands the comb back to Mama. Mama tears off a length of loo paper, and draws it along the teeth of the comb to get rid of the hairs and bits of skin that have accumulated. Then she drops the paper into the pedal bin.

'What do you want me to do now?' asks Granny.

'Here's some moisturiser for your face,' Mama tells her, unscrewing the top of a tub of Nivea. She scoops out a dollop and transfers it onto Granny's fingers.

'What do you want me to *do* with it?'

'Rub it onto your face. You can sit there and do your moisturiser while I tidy up. And then we'll go through to the sitting-room and I'll give you your present.'

'A present? Who's it from?'

'It's from me.'

'Oh! How kind!' Granny proceeds to rub her face with the white cream, pausing to inspect the growth on her jaw with her forefinger. 'I don't like this thing on my face!'

'Try not to fiddle with it, Eleanor. The doctor will have a look at it when Lotus takes you to see him.'

Mama moves to the basin and pulls the plug. The sponge with the shit stains goes into the pedal bin, the flannel is rinsed in hot water and hung on the rail, then Mama washes her hands again and again. She could have OCD, she washes them so thoroughly.

I watch her face in the mirror above the wash-hand basin. Her skin is dull and putty-coloured; dark shadows are scooped beneath her eyes. There is a look of awful resignation in them. I want my lovely Mama back.

After drying her hands on a towel, Mama picks Granny's

discarded nightie up from the floor. I see her inspect it, and as our eyes meet I can tell by her expression that what she's found on the nightie does not fill her with delight. She drops the garment into a plastic bucket and reaches for the long ribbed cardigan that Lotus told her Granny likes to wear in preference to a dressing gown.

Granny has been dabbing her fingers in the tub of Nivea. As Mama reaches out to take it from her, Granny raises a hand and bats at Mama's face, leaving a trail of white cream on her cheek, like war paint. Mama recoils. I know she's been expecting something like this to happen; she's been bookmarking internet sites to do with elder care since she knew she was taking over from Lotus. But it feels shocking, all the same, to see Granny invade Mama's space like this. Mama blinks a couple of times in confusion, as though wondering what tack to take. She clearly decides to ignore the gambit because when she speaks again she uses the upbeat tone of the professional carer.

'Now, Eleanor!' she says. 'Let's go through into the sitting-room, shall we? And then I'll organise lunch for us.'

'Where do you want me to go?' asks Granny.

'The sitting-room.'

'You mumble, you know. It's difficult to hear.'

'Sorry.' Mama helps Granny to her feet. 'Let's get this on first,' she says, holding the cardigan so that Granny can negotiate the sleeves. 'It's nice and warm in here, but it might be a little chillier in the sitting-room. I'll give the central heating a boost.' She moves to the bathroom door and holds it open.

'Where are we going?'

'The sitting-room.'

'Which way is it?'

'It's this way. Follow me.'

Mama starts to walk slowly down the corridor. Granny trails after her, moving like one of the cast members of *The Walking Dead*. When she reaches the turn in the corridor, she halts abruptly.

'Where have the stairs gone?' she asks.

'There are no stairs in this house, Eleanor.'

'Oh, yes. I forgot. There were stairs in my old house, weren't there?'

'Yes.'

'I forget these things, you see.'

'That's because you're very old, Eleanor. It's perfectly natural to forget things at your age.'

Granny sniffs the air. 'What's that smell? Is something burning?'

'No. It's our lunch. We're having macaroni cheese.'

'Oh, good. I love macaroni cheese.'

Mama flicks the booster switch on the wall to reactivate the central heating, then she opens the sitting-room door for Eleanor and we're back in the land of the living. Sunlight is streaming in through the picture windows. Mama's laptop is on the table, with a load of books stacked beside it. I wonder how much work she will manage to do today.

Now, Granny seems to have a better idea of where she's going. She heads towards her armchair like a heat-seeking missile. Well, not *exactly* like a heat-seeking missile, but you know what I mean.

'It's chilly in here,' says Granny.

'I'll put a bar on, until the central heating's warmed up, shall I?' Mama stoops and flicks a switch on the electric fire that sits in front of the big metal fireguard. Then she reaches for a little blue bottle that's sitting on the table beside

Granny's chair. 'Here is your present, Eleanor,' she says.

'Oh! Thank you. What is it?'

'It's a flaçon of scent. *Je Reviens*.' Mama won it in a table quiz quite a long time ago. She tried it for a while, but Dad and I hated it. Dad said it made her smell like somebody he wouldn't want to get to know, so she went back to wearing Chanel No. 5. 'Shall I put some on you?'

'Yes, please. That'd be lovely.'

Mama unscrews the bottle and dabs first Eleanor's left wrist, then her right with perfume. I make a face like an actor in an Ambi-Pur ad and Granny laughs.

'What's it called?' she asks.

'*Je Reviens*.'

'Oh, yes. "I'll be back".'

Like the Terminator.

'Mmm!' says Mama, replacing the stopper. 'How heavenly! We'll have this as a treat every day after your wash, shall we?'

'That'd be lovely! But it's wasted on an old bag like me.'

'You're not an old bag, Eleanor. You're my *belle mere*. That's French for "mother-in-law", you know. It translates as "beautiful mother". Shall I take a photograph of you?'

'Yes.'

How clever Mama is! She's really working hard at keeping Granny sweet. She takes out her phone and holds it at arm's length.

'What are you doing?'

'I'm taking a photograph.'

'Is that a camera?'

'No, it's my phone. Phones can take photographs now, you know.'

'What a lot of nonsense you talk.'

Mama clicks, checks out the image on her screen, then allows herself a smile. Before she sends it off into the ether, I catch a glimpse of the text she's tip-tapped under the screaming face emoji: **Self-portrait after spending a morning with your mother.**

'Now, I'll put your CD player on, so that you can listen to one of your stories before lunch.'

'What are we having?'

'Macaroni cheese. It'll be ready in fifteen minutes.' Mama inserts a CD and, after a moment or two of white noise, a voice booms into the room. '*She's got to be killed!*'

I see a smile play around Mama's lips. She's remembering the Christmas when she and Dad kept corpsing with laughter. 'Is that loud enough for you?'

'No, it's not. Turn it up.'

Mama adjusts the volume to an even higher decibel level, then she says – raising her voice so that she can be heard above the actors bellowing their way through *Appointment with Death* – 'I'll just finish tidying up, then I'll bring lunch in.'

She leaves the room, and I see her demeanour droop a little.

The peacocks are back. They're strutting their stuff about on the lawn. The movement attracts Granny's attention and I see her eyes swivel in the direction of the window. I wonder what she thinks they are, those white shapes? I narrow my eyes so that my vision is blurred. I guess if I were Granny, I might think that there were a couple of small ghosts moseying around the garden. How spooky it must be to live in Granny's world.

From down the corridor, I hear the sound of the garage door being opened. Mama must be putting on a wash – the garage doubles as a laundry room and storage space: there are boxes full of redundant things like cocktail shakers and ashtrays and table linen from the days when Granny used to entertain. I picture Granny sitting at the head of a long table, wearing a little black dress and a string of pearls, smoking a cigarette and laughing at some remark made by one of her guests while Dobby pushes a trolley around the room and serves people crab bisque from a soup tureen.

In Granny's bedroom, the doors to the garden are still open, and the old lady smell is less noticeable. Curious, I move to the bed and have a look. The bottom sheet has a skid-mark on it – it will have to be changed. But there's something worse than the skid-mark. There are bits of Granny on the sheet. Literally. There are flakes of skin and one or two tiny little wart-like things that have parted company from their host.

Mama comes into the room and stands beside me, staring down at the sheet. 'Oh, Katia, oh, Katia,' she says. 'I've never seen anything so gross.'

She pulls the duvet off the bed, then bundles up the sheet and takes it out into the garden, where she shakes it violently. Then she goes back into the garage by the outside door. I see her reach for the stain removal spray on top of the washing machine.

I wonder what Granny's carbon footprint is? Twice a year she spends two or three weeks in my aunt's house in Scotland. And because she can't travel alone, someone has to escort her there and back. So that's eight return flights.

Here in her house, the oil-fired central heating is on and the attic isn't insulated, so there is nothing stopping all the heat just going whishing out through the roof. So much for the double glazing. There are two bars of two electric fires on because Mama forgot to turn off the one in the bathroom.

The washing machine is just about to start a cycle, and then the laundry will have to go into the dryer for ninety minutes or so because there's no washing line in any of Granny's four gardens because Granny says washing lines look common. The immersion heater is on, and the fridge freezer and the oven, and after lunch the dishwasher will go into action. *Appointment with Death* is running on electricity, and if Mama puts Granny in front of a David Attenborough DVD this afternoon two more electrical appliances will be roped into play.

Dad wrote an article about carbon footprinting a couple of years ago. He worked out that, as a family, we were doing OK because there are only three of us. Did you know that the average family in the UK emits ten tons of carbon dioxide every year? And that a return flight from London to the Maldives gives off 2.3 tonnes per passenger?

It's amazing to think that one little old lady's emissions are higher than those of a family of four who take a foreign holiday twice a year.

7

A HANDSOME PRINCE

Lunch was a pallid affair. Literally. Macaroni cheese was not such a great idea because it was the same colour as the plate, and Mama had to keep spearing bits of macaroni for Granny. And every time she did it, Granny would ask what was on the fork. Mama must have said the words 'macaroni cheese' about twenty times. And then Granny sneezed, and Mama did not eat any more of her lunch because some of the sneeze went on her plate.

Granny's in the Brown Study now, ensconced in front of the cricket on telly, and Mama's back at work in the sitting-room. I'm up a tree!

It's in the next-door neighbours' garden, but I'm not really trespassing because the house is up for sale again and there's no one living here. We never got to know the last people who lived here (Granny took against them because they drove a Nissan), but we were quite friendly with the family before that. They were called the Robinsons, and it was them who raised the alarm about Granny's dementia. Mrs Robinson saw Granny's handbag sitting on the bench outside the open front door early one morning and phoned Dad to warn him.

Dad worked out that the bag had been there all night, and that meant the door had been open all night, too, because the bench had been the last place he'd seen Granny before he'd driven away.

The Robinsons had a son who was two years older than me. He was called Mark and we used to play together any time I came out with Dad. At first Mark pretended he was too cool to play with a girl two years younger than him, but eventually he decided that anyone was better than no one – he was an only child, too – and we ended up getting on quite well.

Mark's dad built him a tree house, and that's where I am now. It's a really cool tree house because it's practically invisible – especially at this time of the year, when the trees are in leaf. The floor is a wooden platform, but the walls are made from what Mark's dad called 'osier'. Osier is a type of willow that's used in wickerwork because the branches are dead flexible. Mark's dad wove the osier into a kind of beehive shape, like a pod, and then he covered it in camouflage material, and Mark and I got loads of sticks and branches and attached them to the camouflage. If you spotted the tree house from the road, you might think it is actually a heron's nest, it's that good. Bear Grylls would envy it.

When Mark got a new PlayStation he stopped coming to the osier pod, but I loved that I had the place to myself. I'd climb up here with my books and my art stuff and talk to a spider I named after the heroine of *Charlotte's Web*. She had spun a spectacular web between the ribs of the osier pod, and when Mama heard me chattering away she told me it felt like eavesdropping on a private conversation.

From here, I can see Mama sitting at the table in the sitting-room. She has her concentrating face on, and her fingers are fairly flying across the keyboard. As I was passing the table earlier, I took a look at a book that she had left lying open at the index page. It was a book on writing, and the chapter headings were all pompy, like 'The Writer, the Reader, and the Book as Go-Between' and 'At Whose Altar should the Writer Worship?' and other such shite.

I wish Mama wasn't writing grip lit, even if it is the new big thing in publishing. I wish she was writing something that would make her laugh. She used to laugh a lot at her own stuff when she worked as a copywriter. That's because she was really good at it – one of her ads was nominated for a BTAA commercial of the year.

Somewhere, someone's started up a lawnmower. I open my eyes. Mama is no longer at the table in the sitting-room. She must have gone to get Granny her cup of tea: I can tell by the position of the sun in the sky that it's around four o'clock. She comes back into the room just as a lad with a motor mower rounds the corner. Granny's carbon footprint just got heavier.

Mama looks through the window, then she opens it and leans out.

'Hi,' she says; but the lad can't hear her over the noise of the lawnmower, so '*Hi!*' she calls again, in the louder voice she has to remember to use for Granny.

The lad kills the engine. 'Hi,' he says, ambling towards the window. He looks a lot like the picture of the prince in my old illustrated copy of *The Little Mermaid*, with green eyes and wavy, shoulder-length brown hair.

I often wondered about the green eyes in the illustration, because in the story the little mermaid says that the prince's eyes are black. But I suppose black eyes might look spooky in a colour illustration, like the way Granny's eyes go all stony when she stares.

In any photographs taken of Granny in the last ten years, she looks as if she's been added on as a digital afterthought. There's a framed photograph in the Brown Study that was taken one Christmas at my aunt's house. It's a big family photograph, and everyone is wearing paper hats and wide smiles. Granny is wearing a paper hat too, but no smile. She has a lost look about her, as if she hasn't a clue what is going on around her: which, of course, she hasn't.

Mama's leant her elbows on the windowsill and is smiling at the brown-haired lad. 'I assume you're not mowing the lawn out of the goodness of your heart,' she says.

''Fraid not. I've been covering for my dad since he did his back in.'

'Your dad is George, the gardener?'

'That's right.' The lad smiles and sticks out his hand. 'And you're Tess, right?'

'Right.'

'I'm Toby. Lotus said you were taking over for a while. How are you getting on?'

'Fine.'

You don't tell people the truth when they ask questions like that, do you? Imagine if Mama had said, 'Well, Mrs E threw a spoon and yelled at me this morning and then I had to clean her shitty arse and change her shitty sheets and feed her macaroni while she sneezed all over my lunch.' You just *don't* tell people the truth.

I wonder how many women of Mama's age are doing exactly what she's doing, without getting paid for it? I wonder how many forty- and fifty- and even sixty-something women are caring for their parents? Maybe loads of these women have just finished rearing a family and have been looking forward to their new-found freedom. Maybe loads of them got pregnant late in life thanks to IVF and are still bringing up small children? And maybe in the not-too-distant future – now that there's a new miracle drug that they say will postpone the menopause – fifty-something-year-old women will be breastfeeding their babies and spoon-feeding their mothers at the same time?

I wonder how many knackered women slump in front of the television every night and watch travel programmes where 'silver foxes' go on Saga cruises, or have makeovers done that 'take ten years off' their lives? I wonder how many women zap off Davina McCall when she grins at them from the screen, giving the UltraLift Challenge to those who simply haven't the energy or the money to grow old disgracefully? There must be nothing more sick-making than watching shiny, happy people on the telly when your life's gone down the pan.

Mama has taken her wallet out of her handbag. 'I may as well pay you now,' she tells Toby. 'What's the damage?'

'It's twenty quid for an hour.'

'Twenty quid an *hour*? Sheesh! I'd do it for that. How long will the job take?'

'I should be finished in two if you want me to tidy up by the pond as well.'

Mama peels off two twenties and hands them to Toby through the window.

'Thanks,' he says, sticking the money in the back pocket of his jeans. He nods towards Mama's laptop. 'The noise won't disturb you, will it?'

She shakes her head. 'No, the windows are double-glazed.'

'Catch you later,' says Toby.

I watch as he strolls back across the lawn. Twenty quid an hour to mow Granny's lawn! Dad's more or less given up on our garden. It used to be really pretty, but keeping it that way was costing too much money, and now he's lost all interest in it. I heard him tell Mama that there'd be no hanging baskets this year, not just because of the money but because gardening doesn't make him happy any more, the way it used to.

It was too much information for me.

Do you know something? I sometimes think that my parents imagine that just because I cannot talk doesn't mean I cannot hear. I hear *everything*. Katia is all ears.

And now my ears are buzzing with the mowing. It's quite a soothing sound – kind of like an electronic lullaby; it recedes and draws nearer, recedes and draws nearer . . .

8

HOW TO KNIT A VELOCIRAPTOR

The mowing noise stops altogether. Toby is coming round the corner of the house with a pile of cuttings for the composter. He's taken off his shirt and he looks like one of *Heat* magazine's torsos of the week. I'd love a statue of him to replace the redundant heron. The little mermaid kept a statue of the prince in her underwater garden. Her garden was circular, planted with only red flowers because she wanted it to look like the sun – like the sun she only ever saw when she broke through the waves.

The composter is directly below the tree I'm sitting in, but on the other side of the hedge. As Toby slings the cuttings into it, the branches of Granny's cherry tree make a soughing sound and some blossom floats down and lands on his head. I stifle a snigger. He looks up. Our eyes meet. But I know he can't see me. I am too well camouflaged in my beehive hut.

In the sitting-room I see Mama get to her feet and stretch. She opens the window and calls, 'Hey – Toby!'

'Ma'am?'

Oh! I love that he calls her 'Ma'am'! There's something so old-fashioned and charming about it.

'Please – call me Tess. D'you fancy a beer after your exertions?'

'I'd love one.'

Mama leaves the sitting-room and reappears a minute later with two cans. Toby pulls on his T-shirt and joins her on the bench by the front door. I'd love to sit down with them, but I'm too shy. Mama knows that I'm always awestruck when I'm in the company of handsome men. She introduced me to Benedict Cumberbatch once, when he was doing some voice-over work for an ad she had written, and I couldn't meet his eyes. His eyes are so mesmeric that I knew that if I looked into them I would be like the rabbit locking eyes with a snake: I totally would not be able to look away. So I just mumbled something incoherent and went all red. Lola would have flirted. She enjoys being the centre of attention. I sometimes wonder how two such different people as Lola and me became such good friends.

I slide out of my osier cocoon and back down the tree. There's a gap in the hedge between the Robinsons' garden and Granny's, so I shimmy through and go round the side of the house, where I can sit on my hunkers and listen to Mama and Toby talking. He's telling her about the law course he's doing at uni and how he wants to run for president of the Students' Union next year. He's ambitious! He has – as they say – prospects.

'Are you a full-time writer?' he asks Mama.

'I'd like to be. That's why I've come out here – for some peace and quiet.'

Mama's being economical with the truth. But I guess she can't very well tell a complete stranger that she's come out here because she's been made redundant and desperately needs the money that caring for Granny is going to bring in.

'Peace and quiet is right. Apart from those effing peacocks. They'd give you the heebie-jeebies. The first time I heard them I thought a baby was being murdered.'

'Who owns them?'

'Mrs Greeve, down the road. Do you know her?'

'I don't know anyone around here.'

'I notice you've no car.'

'My husband needs it, in town.'

'How do you get by, with no transport?'

'I did a big shop before I came here. We'll do another one at the weekend, when Donn comes, and there's always the service station down the road if I run out of essentials. They do a great line in cuddly toys and dead flowers.'

'Jesus. I'd go mental, stuck out here with no car.'

'Makes no odds to me. I don't drive.'

'You don't *drive*?'

'No. I was in a – I was in an accident, once, and lost my nerve.'

'A car accident?'

'I don't talk about it.'

There's a pause. I hear Toby take a swig of his beer, then he says, 'Bit of a waste of money, isn't it – doing Mrs Ellis's garden?'

'What do you mean?'

'Well, she can't see it, can she? So what difference does it make whether the lawn's mowed or not?'

'That's a tough one to answer.'

'What age is she now?'

'Nearly ninety, and suckin' diesel, as they say. I'd say she has another decade to go.'

'You think she'll hit the ton?'

'Yes, I do.'

Toby takes another swig. 'It's funny . . . you keep hearing that people are living longer, but you don't see really old people around much, do you?'

'Do you mean in public?'

'Yeah.'

'They're family secrets. Kept in cupboards, like skeletons.'

'Seriously. Where are they all?'

'You see them in the usual places, like the Botanic Gardens or National Trust properties at the weekends, when they're wheeled out for a jolly. Except nobody ever looks jolly. Everybody looks like they should be in Banksy's Dismaland.'

'Do you take Mrs E on jollies?'

'We used to. But she finds it an awful strain now. So do we. Even getting her dressed and into the car takes some doing. And any time we go into a restaurant, people stare. The last time we took her to lunch a toddler burst into tears.'

'Why?'

'Because she looks such a fright. The child probably thought she was a witch.'

'Jesus. I hope I never get to be that old.'

'I repeat that every day, like a mantra. And then I find myself doing "old" type stuff.'

'Like what?'

'Like criticising the girls on *Big Brother* for lewd behaviour.'

Toby gives her a curious look. 'I'd never have taken you for the kind of person who watches *Big Brother*.'

'I'm an addict. I find it completely riveting.'

It's true. I remember the first time Mama watched *Big Brother*. She was zapping though the channels trying to find a documentary about the pre-Raphaelites when she hit on it. One of the contestants was throwing a tantrum in the Diary Room and Mama simply could not believe what she was seeing. She stood there with the zapper in her hand for five minutes, then she sat down on the edge of the coffee table; then, during the break, she poured herself a glass of wine and curled up on the sofa and watched right through to the end. From then on in, she was hooked.

'I've never understood the appeal,' says Toby.

'It's the Diary Room that fascinates me,' says Mama. 'I love the idea of a cocoon where people can confide their troubles to a disembodied voice. A kind of benign guru.'

'There are helplines for that.'

'There's only so much a helpline volunteer can do.'

Mama knows what she's talking about. Any time she tried helplines after the accident she always got different people on the other end. That meant she had to explain her problem over and over and over again until she couldn't bear it any more. And while the helpline people were well meaning and sympathetic – *really* sympathetic – they could not *empathise* because they had not been through what Mama had been through. There's a big difference between empathy and sympathy. And Big Brother really does empathise with the housemates because Big Brother knows and understands what is going on all the time in the house.

From the sitting-room, through the open window comes the sound of the carriage clock chiming.

'Is that six o'clock already?' says Mama, getting up from the bench. 'I promised Eleanor I'd go into her at six on the button.'

'I'll be off then,' says Toby. 'Thanks for the beer.'

'You're welcome. It was nice to have a sane person to talk to.'

Um – hel*lo*?! You talk to me all the time! I may not talk back, Mama, but I'm a good listener.

I watch as Toby moves to the gate and unlatches it. As he passes through, I see his eyes go to the tree where the beehive hut is. Did he sense I was there, earlier? I feel like the little mermaid, when she spied unseen on the prince. I wonder . . . I wonder . . . If the little mermaid had known that he would never return her love, would she have sacrificed her fish tail and her lovely voice?

What made stupid Disney change the ending? Did they think that children couldn't handle the truth? That shit doesn't happen? Some of the very best stories have tragic endings. *The Velveteen Rabbit. The Fault in Our Stars. The Boy in the Striped Pyjamas. The Happy Prince. Charlotte's Web. Charlotte's Web!* The last line of the second-to-last chapter goes, 'No one was with her when she died.' How harrowing is that?

In the kitchen Mama has poured herself a large gin and she's rubbing a trace of Gordon's around the rim of Granny's glass of tonic.

I give her a complicit smile and we go into the Brown Study.

'It's six o'clock, Eleanor – and I'm finished work for the day!' breezes Mama. 'Thank goodness for that!'

'What were you doing?'

'I'm working on a novel, Eleanor, on my laptop computer. I'm going to be doing that every afternoon. But on the dot of six o'clock, when I hear the carriage clock chime, I'm going to stop and call it a day.'

'Right-oh.'

'Here's a nice G&T for you.' Mama sets the glass down and aims the channel-changer at the telly. 'Let's watch the news, shall we?'

First up is the story of the child who's gone missing.

'Oh – it's terribly sad, isn't it?' says Mama. 'That poor little girl is still missing.'

'Who is missing?'

'A little girl has gone missing. She was on holiday with her parents.'

'That's dreadful! *How* did she go missing?'

'It looks like she might have wandered out of the apartment complex they were staying in and was abducted.'

'Abducted by whom?'

'Nobody knows.'

'That's dreadful! Someone should report it.'

'It's been reported, Eleanor, don't worry. There's an investigation going on now.'

'An investigation?'

'By the police.'

'You're telling me that someone took the child?'

'Yes. It looks like it.'

'*How* did they take her?'

'While her parents were playing tennis.'

'Outside?'

Mama sighs. 'Yes.'

'Then what did they expect? You don't go off and play tennis and leave your child on its own, do you?'

'Well, they didn't really go *off* anywhere. The tennis court was in the same complex, you see, and their little girl—'

But Granny doesn't let Mama finish. She wants to be able to give out. 'What did they expect? Honestly. How irresponsible! They had no business to go waltzing off to tennis like that without the child.'

'The child was under supervision, Eleanor, in a play area. It wasn't as if they abandoned her.'

'Well, they won't be doing that again in a hurry, will they? They've learned their lesson now.'

'Excuse me for a minute, Eleanor. I just want to check on something in the kitchen.'

Mama gets abruptly to her feet, picks up her glass and leaves the room. In the kitchen, she takes a swig of gin, then covers her eyes with her hand.

'Oh, fuck. Oh, fuck, Katia. I can't bear it.'

The phone rings. It's Dad.

'Oh – Donn! Hello, hello!' Mama's voice is shaky.

'What's up?'

'I was watching the news with Eleanor and she started giving out stink about the parents of that poor little girl who's gone missing. I don't think I can take it.' Mama starts to cry.

'Hush, hush. There, there. Hush, hush.' Dad carries on saying 'hush, hush' and 'there, there' for many more moments until Mama's sobs have calmed down and she's at the hiccupping stage. Then he says, 'Hang in there, darling. You're bound to feel fragile after your first day. Once you've got a routine established, things will get easier. You've just got to stay strong.'

Mama snuffles in response. 'I feel like such a wimp. I was courageous once, and outgoing. Now I'm scared of an old lady.'

'Maybe watching the news is not such a good idea. It's full of stuff she can be negative about.'

'You're right.' I see Mama's eyes go to a magazine on top of a pile that Lotus has made. It's folded over at an article entitled 'How to Make a Découpage Tray'. 'I guess I could start doing activities with her instead.'

'What kind of activities?'

Mama starts leafing through the magazine. 'How to Make a Tote Bag'. 'How to Make a Dog Coat'. 'How to Make a Macramé Plant Hanger'.

'I'm looking at some in a magazine. They all seem a bit ambitious. "Knit Your Own Velociraptor".'

'Are you serious?'

'Yes, I am. Listen, here's how to do the teeth. "With sn make approx. 17 2-loop French knots."'

'What's "sn"?'

'I haven't a clue.' Mama turns another page. 'Or we could make a charming needle felted dog.'

'And enter it for the Turner prize.'

'I think I'll stick to the kind of activities the internet sites suggest. Crosswords, photograph albums – that kind of stuff. I found an old album, by the way. Full of photographs and press cuttings about Eleanor in her acting days. I'll sit down and go through it with her this evening.'

'She'd love that.'

'I need help here. *I need help!*' It's Granny's voice, coming from the Brown Study.

'Hang on a sec, Donn.' Mama swings out of the kitchen, into the study, where Granny is scowling at the television screen. 'What is it, Eleanor?' she asks.

'*I can't hear it.*'

'Oh.'

Mama goes to pick up the remote, which has fallen to the floor, and as she does so Granny raises a hand and grabs hold of Mama's hair.

'Ow! What are you *doing*, Eleanor?'

Mama jerks away, and her plait of hair slips from Granny's grasp. She takes a step back and she and Granny glare at each other for a moment. Then Mama aims the remote at the telly gunslinger-style before dropping it onto a pouffe and leaving the room.

'She wanted the sound on the telly turned up,' she says into the phone.

'I heard.'

'She pulled my hair.'

'Did she hurt you?'

'No. I just got a bit of a fright.'

There's a silence, and I know there's no point in Mama telling Dad how grim things are because he knows.

'I have a joke for you,' she says instead. 'I got it on the internet this afternoon.'

'Shoot.'

'At the age of ninety-three, Mildred was left a widow. She decided to end it all and join her husband in death, so to make sure she did the job properly, she phoned her doctor and asked exactly where the human heart is. He told her that it's just behind the left breast. So Mildred took her husband's revolver, placed it with precision and fired. Half an hour later she was admitted to hospital with a gunshot wound to her left knee.'

Dad laughs. 'Bye, Tess.'

'Bye, Donn. Love you.'

'I love you, too.'

And I love you both. I smile.

Mama puts the phone down and moves to the freezer. It's well stocked with Tesco's Finest because Granny has always insisted on it. 'I always insist on the finest.' She used to say it in a mock-autocratic way, but one day it stopped being even mildly funny. Mama reaches for a chicken and mushroom pie and slides it into the microwave, then she sits down at the table in the breakfast room to peruse a back issue of Lotus's

Red magazine while she waits for dinner to defrost.

In the Brown Study, Granny is happily sipping at her tonic water. The news item on the telly is to do with the ageing demographic.

'The Government is simply not prepared for this demographic time bomb,' a pundit is saying. 'By 2030 there will be nearly five million more people over the age of sixty-five living in Britain – that's a fifty per cent increase, with a one hundred per cent increase in over eighty-fives. The incidence of dementia is forecast to increase by eighty per cent, while cases of arthritis, heart disease and stroke will rise by fifty per cent.'

Maths has always been my worst subject, but even I can see that these figures are insane.

'Living for longer is to be celebrated,' continues the pundit, 'but it generates economic challenges for health and social services now dealing with chronic illnesses that would previously have reduced life expectancy . . .'

I slide a look at Granny, wondering if she has taken any of this in, but her eyes are fixed on the window.

'There's a penguin, Katia!' she says. 'That was a penguin, you know. I saw it land on the windowsill. And then it took off. It was a penguin.'

9

THE OSIER POD

'Salutations, Charlotte! It's been a while.'

'Salutations, Katia! I've been expecting you. How are you today?'

'I'm doing OK, thank you kindly. And you?'

'I'm a little tired. I have been working on my web since sunrise, with just one small bug for sustenance.'

'That's not good, Charlotte. You must keep up your strength.'

'There's another in my larder. I've been saving it. Now, down to business. By my calculations, this is your fifth day in the house. I understand that you have some concerns. Would you like to share them, Katia?'

'Yes, I would. I'm worried about Mama.'

'Why are you worried?'

'She's not eating properly. She finds it hard to eat when she's stressed, and I think that having to sit at the same table as Granny is putting her off her food even more.'

'How is the mood in the house, otherwise?'

'Middling good, I guess. Mama has finally got a routine going. Granny likes her, even though she mostly hasn't a clue who she is. But it's hard work – really hard work. Not just the cooking and cleaning and washing and that, but mentally. It's not good for Mama's head. And I'll probably go out of my mind with boredom soon. So we'll all three be living in a loony bin.'

'That's a very politically incorrect term, Katia. We must be careful. We don't want to cause offence.'

'By using politically incorrect language?'

'Indeed. My own story was banned in the state of Kansas just a decade ago.'

'*Charlotte's Web* was *banned*? Why?'

'The theme of death was deemed inappropriate subject matter for a children's book.'

'So what am I meant to say instead of "loony"?'

'Granny might be described as having a personality disorder.'

'A personality disorder? She has dementia, for fuck's sake! Sorry for saying "fuck", Charlotte.'

'Granny did not always have dementia, Katia. She was once good and kind and fun-loving.'

'I know. I know! Dad's forever going on about how good and kind and fun-loving she was. But I never knew her when she was like that. I've only ever known her as the witch.'

'You must realise that your father loves Granny very much.'

'Yeah, I do. But I heard him tell Mama that he's finding it more and more difficult to love her.'

'Why is that, Katia?'

'He's finding it more and more difficult to remember her as she was. And I know that he'd go crazy if she did anything to hurt Mama.'

'You are aware that Donn and your aunt Gemma want to

keep Granny in her own house for as long as possible?'

'Yes.'

'So what do you think should happen to Granny now, Katia?'

'I think she should go into a home.'

'That will be very difficult for your father. He and Gemma decided that it was best for Granny to stay here until she dies, surrounded by the things she knows and loves.'

'But she doesn't know or love anything or anyone now. She doesn't know where she is, or what day it is. It could be December 1984, for all she knows. And she doesn't know what Mama is doing here.'

'Why do you think Granny should go into a home, Katia?'

'Because soon she won't be able to get out of bed. And then she will get bedsores. And she'll probably become incontinent, and what'll happen then? Lotus told Mama that Granny won't wear nappies, and Lotus and Mama can't carry on looking after her forever. We will need what they call "Healthcare Professionals" – not just a minder like Lotus – and they will cost a bomb, and Dad and Gemma will have to sell the house.'

'Has Granny ever had occasion to stay in a home before?'

'Yes. When Lotus had to go back to Malaysia when her father was dying and there was no one to look after Granny. That was in the days when Mama still had a job.'

'Did you ever visit Granny in the home, Katia?'

'Yes.'

'And what did you think of it?'

'I thought it was horrendous.'

'Why was it horrendous?'

'It was full of old ladies all sitting on chairs, in rows, watching *Deal or No Deal*. Except they weren't really watching it. They were just staring into the middle distance. And the room smelled of canteen food and wee, and some of the old ladies – they were nearly all women, you know – were wearing bibs and being spoon-fed their lunch. And when we came in, Granny thought we had come to spring her and she looked so relieved, and then Dad had to tell her that no, we hadn't come to spring her, we'd just come for a visit, and Granny cried and Dad cried too, in the car on the way home. He just sat in the car park behind the wheel of the car and cried and cried.'

'It must have been very painful for him.'

'Yes, it was.'

'So putting Granny in a home would be the last resort.'

'Yeah. But you know something, Charlotte? I don't care any more. I don't care because Mama and Dad are more important to me than Granny. And Dad is stressed because he thinks his paper might go under and he'll be out of a job, and Mama is stressed because she's finding looking after Granny so tough, and she's been working so hard on this novel – any time she's not doing things for Granny she's at her computer. And the worst thing of all is . . .'

'Yes, Katia? What is the worst thing of all?'

'The worst thing of all is that I don't think the novel is very good.'

'What makes you say that, Katia?'

'Well, sometimes I stand behind her while she's working, and she's so absorbed in her writing that she doesn't notice I'm there, and I read bits of it over her shoulder. And – oh! I feel so disloyal saying this, but it's – it's stilted.'

'Why is it stilted?'

'She uses words that people would never say in real life. Like today she put in a description of a tree, and she called

79

it "venerable". I mean, who would ever look at a tree and call it "venerable"? You'd just call it "big", wouldn't you? And the dialogue is embarrassing – all full of, like, "dude" and "muthafucka".'

'What kind of book is Tess writing, Katia?'

'It's a thriller.'

'Street talk features a lot in thrillers. What's the storyline?'

'It's about a little girl who goes missing.'

'That's hard.'

'Yes.'

'But it's a popular subject. Think of all the best-sellers today that have "Missing" in the title.'

'It's never going to be a best-seller. It won't even find a publisher. It's crap. Mama's book is crap, Charlotte.'

'You really are very worried about her, aren't you, Katia?'

'Yes.'

'Have you got a handkerchief, Katia?'

'No.'

'Then wipe your nose on your sleeve.'

'OK. Sorry. Sorry about this.'

'Don't worry, Katia.'

'There's something else, Charlotte. She's – she's drinking too much. She's started to have a glass of wine with her lunch – except she hardly eats any lunch. And then it's a gin and tonic at six o'clock, and then wine with dinner – except she hardly eats any dinner either – and more wine until she comes to bed. I'm always in bed before her, and sometimes she doesn't even bother to say goodnight. And one night she fell asleep in the chair and came to bed hours later without cleaning her teeth.'

'How do you know that she didn't clean her teeth, Katia?'

'There was no smell of toothpaste on her breath. There

was only a wine smell. I've never known Mama to go to bed without cleaning her teeth, ever. She's fastidious about personal hygiene. And that's something else that's making life here so grim for her, because Granny is really unhygienic. You know she peed on the carpet in the hall the other day, and some of it went into her slippers, and Mama had to throw the slippers out. And I don't know what it is about the smell of Granny's wee, but it really is gross. I think it's because she drinks hardly any water, only apple juice. I thought that Mama was going to throw up the other day when she washed Granny. She gagged twice.'

'Why do you think Tess is drinking so much, Katia?'

'Because she's truly miserable. I haven't seen her so miserable since the accident.'

'She's drowning her sorrows.'

'Yes. But it's not just sorrow.'

'What else is Tess feeling? Take as long as you need, Katia. I know this is difficult for you.'

'She's feeling scared.'

'What is she scared of?'

'She's scared of Granny. She's started locking our bedroom door at night because Granny moves around the house and sticks her head into all the rooms to check on who's there.'

'It must be scary for Granny, too. It must be very scary to wake up in the middle of the night and not have any idea as to whether or not you are alone in a house.'

'Yes, yes, I know. But I think it's worse to be in Mama's shoes. Granny's like one of those cranky old dogs – the kind that turn round and give you a nip for no reason.'

'Are you thinking of the time she pulled Tess's hair?'

'Yes. And I saw her blow her nose on Mama's scarf and it was deliberate, you know? And she talks to dead people. She talks to my granddad. And she talks to her mother. Mama heard her talking the other day, and when she went to look, Granny had the phone up against her ear and she was talking to her mother. "Goodbye then, Mother. I hope you have a pleasant evening. I'll come and visit some time soon." That's what she was saying, as normal as I'm talking to you. And sometimes she appears out of nowhere, like a zombie. Remember when Mama was talking to a friend on the phone the other day – pacing up and down on the terrace, the way she does – and Granny appeared?'

'Yes.'

'Well, I tried to warn her that Granny was coming —'

'How did you try to warn her?'

'I made the scuba sign for danger.'

'What is the scuba sign for danger, Katia? Can you demonstrate for me?'

'You make your hand into a fist and punch it out straight in front of you, like this. But Mama didn't see in time, and when she turned around, there was Granny standing in her nightie in the sun porch, and Mama literally screamed with fright.'

'You must help Tess be strong, Katia.'

'Well, that's why I'm here. For moral support.'

'Things will improve tomorrow, when Donn comes to visit. And after the weekend, there will be only two more weeks to go. Between the pair of you, you'll get there.'

'I wish there was more I could do for Mama. I feel awfully helpless. I wish I could talk to her.'

'You're doing everything you can, Katia. I'm watching. And remember – I see everything.'

'Of course.'

'I have seen your concern for Tess and I've decided that it should be rewarded.'

'How?'

'I have petitioned the Dream Spinner for some quality Dream Time you can share with Tess.'

'The Dream Spinner! Yay! What did he say?'

'The Dream Spinner has granted my request. Between the hours of three and five o'clock, you may visit Tess in a dream and talk to her.'

'Oh! You rock, Charlotte! Thank you so much!'

'You are welcome, Katia. But there is one condition.'

'Yes?'

'You must not speak to Tess about anything that may upset or trouble her. That will topple your precious Dream Time into nightmare. Do you understand?'

'I understand. I will be sure to only talk about nice things, to make her Dream Time happy. I might tell her a story.'

'That would be lovely, Katia. Oh! Forgive me for yawning. You may now leave the Osier Pod. I am in need of a nap.'

'It was so good to talk to you – just like in the old days! I feel so much better. Thank you.'

'Goodbye, Katia. Take care.'

'I will. Sleep tight, Charlotte.'

10

HAPPILY EVER AFTER

Ding! Ding! Ding!

The carriage clock strikes three: the Dream Spinner has kept his promise. I slide into Mama's dream from above. She's sitting at a steel table in the centre of a box-hedge maze that stretches as far as the eye can see. Her laptop is open in front of her and she's tip-tapping away.

'Hello, Mama,' I say.

'Hello, darling,' she replies abstractedly.

'Is this a bad time? I don't want to disturb you, if the words are flowing.'

'No, no! I'm just finishing something . . . there!' She turns to me, and smiles. 'How are you, sweetheart?'

'I'm good. How's your novel going?'

She pulls her legs up onto the seat of her steel chair and hugs her knees to her chest. 'It's getting there – it really is. I have a feeling about this book, Katia. I think it's going to be a winner.'

'Of course it will be a winner! You're a brilliant writer! You've won awards!'

Mama smiles her crooked smile. 'Writing advertising copy is very different to writing a novel, kitten.'

'It's still about writing good words. Just more of them.'

'I wish it was as simple as that.'

A small hippopotamus comes trundling around the corner of the box hedge. I'm about to say, 'Holy crap! How did that get here?' when I remember we're in a dream. 'Shoo!' says Mama, and the hippopotamus retreats.

'Do you know the ending yet?' I ask her. 'Is it happy or sad?'

'I haven't decided. I'd love it to be happy, but market trends say endings should be downbeat these days – especially in grip lit.' She types, enters, clicks and scrolls down an Amazon page of best-selling titles. 'Look. Look at all these dark jackets. Gone are the days of sugared-almond shades of blue and pink.'

'I think it's a shame. I used to love the feeling I got when you finished up my bedtime stories with the words, "And they all lived happily ever after." Stephenie Meyer says she loves happy endings because they're so rare.'

'Who's Stephenie Meyer?'

'She wrote the *Twilight* books. She's a multi-multimillionaire now.'

'Hmm. The fantasy trend was—'

'Forget trends. If you could write anything – anything at all, Mama – what would it be?'

'Historical. But nobody's buying historical novels any more.'

'What *is* selling, then – apart from grip lit?'

'Memoir. Look.' Mama clicks again, and a load of best-selling memoirs shimmer onto the screen.

'Bloody hell. Stephen Fry's written three. You should

give it a go. You could write a brilliant memoir.'

I can't unsay it.

Mama's brow puckers, her fingers clench into a fist and her knuckles go white. 'Don't be so stupid, Katia,' she says.

What did Charlotte say? 'You must not speak to Tess about anything that may upset or trouble her. That will topple your precious Dream Time into nightmare . . .' *Change the subject change the subject change the subject, Katia, quick . . .*

I will the hippopotamus to come back; I will Granny to wake up; I will something – anything – to happen that will bring Mama back to the here and now.

'Tell me – tell me about when I was a baby,' I say, on impulse.

It works. Mama's expression softens. 'Oh, you were the most beautiful, darling thing!' she says.

'Dad says I looked like the baby in *Alice in Wonderland* who turns into a pig.'

'Don't listen to him! He'd never seen a newborn before. Neither had I, come to think of it. We were utterly clueless about parenting. Until you came along, I don't think I'd ever held a baby in my life.'

Hold me . . .

'Let's have a cuddle! Let's turn that horrible steel chair into a sofa, so we can cuddle up and tell each other stories, like we did in the old days.'

'Turn the chair into a sofa? What are you *on*, Katia?'

'It's a dream. We can do anything we like in dreams.'

'Oh. Right.'

And suddenly we're snuggled up on the sofa in the sitting-room at home. It's all draped with velvety throws and plump with cushions, and Mama's purple cashmere shawl is swathed around us. It smells of Chanel No. 5 and we're

86

looking at the picture in *Alice in Wonderland* of Alice holding the bottle labelled 'DRINK ME'. And then Mama starts to read.

"'It might end, you know," said Alice to herself, "in my going out altogether, like a candle. I wonder what I should be like then?" And she tried to fancy what the flame of a candle looks like after the candle is blown out, for she could not remember ever having seen such a thing . . .'

And for the rest of Dream Time, Mama and I stay curled up together on the couch, reading *Alice in Wonderland*.

As the carriage clock chimes a tinny five o'clock, Mama reaches the bit where the Mad Hatter and the March Hare are stuffing the Dormouse into the teapot. She is engrossed in the story. I slip discreetly out of the dream, refocus my eyes to get accustomed to the dimness of the bedroom, then look down at Mama's sleeping face. She's snuggled up to Teddy, and she's smiling.

11

THE RING OF DOOM

Yay! It's Saturday. We have got through a whole week in the Gingerbread House and Dad is due any minute. Mama has washed her hair and spritzed herself with eau de parfum and slicked on a little lip gloss, and she's singing along to Bob Marley. She even laughed at something on Facebook today.

It's another beautiful day. The lawn is littered with blossom and the birdsong is boisterous (apart from the white peacocks, who have left off their caterwauling, thank goodness). And now Dad's car is coming through the gates that Mama opened for him earlier, and Mama is running out and waving, and I blow him loads of kisses as he gets out of the car and do a little dance for joy.

'Come, come quickly,' says Mama. 'Let's sneak up and sit by the pond, and we'll have each other to ourselves before Eleanor realises you're here and gets jealous.'

We climb the steps, and I climb further still, up the bank to where a silver poplar grows. It has a kind of hollow in the roots, and I always imagined a hobbit might live there. I used to nestle in that hollow with a book when I was younger, and I remember Dad always used to put the last egg there in the hunt he'd do for me any time we had to spend Easter at Granny's. It was always the biggest and best one, and we'd save it for after dinner, when Mama would put on a DVD of *Easter Parade* and watch it with Granny while Dad and I played *Tomb Raider* and pigged out on chocolate.

I nearly died when I was watching *Tomb Raider* once. I used to wear an Irish Claddagh ring, and I had a habit of putting it in my mouth and sucking on it. Mama used to give out yards because it was unhygienic. And then one day, when Dad and me were playing *Tomb Raider*, Lara Croft went round a corner and two big black dogs jumped out at her, and I got such a fright that I fell off my stool and the Claddagh ring got stuck in my windpipe. Mama always said afterwards that she would never ever forget the sound I made. It made her drop the glass she was drying and race up the stairs to my bedroom, taking the steps three at a time. Dad got hold of me from behind and did the Heimlich manoeuvre, and the ring came shooting back out of my mouth. It was lucky that Dad had the skill to do the Heimlich manoeuvre because otherwise I'd have been dead within minutes, no word of a lie. And Mama took the Claddagh Ring of Doom and threw it in the bin, and I haven't worn a stitch of jewellery since.

Dad learned the Heimlich manoeuvre when he was doing his Rescue Diver training. That's the cool thing about scuba diving – you get to learn loads of skills. Dad's an Emergency First Responder. So am I. It was the first speciality course I did after I got my Open Water certification.

The other speciality course I did was dry suit diving. Dry suits are the ones that do exactly what it says on the tin: they keep you dry. You wear a kind of onesie underneath, called a 'woolly bear', and that keeps you toasty in cold water. You could even wear a tux underneath, James Bond style!

You don't need dry suits in places like Jamaica, of course, because the water is so warm, but on the west coast of Scotland, where there is some brilliant diving, you really do need a dry suit. Somebody once told Mama that loads of divers pee into their wetsuits when they get into the water to warm themselves up, so Mama swore she would never get into a rental wetsuit ever again. That's when she insisted on all three of us buying our own dry suits.

She and Dad are sitting on the bench below me, holding hands, and Mama is telling him about the beetle she found on her bedroom floor this morning. I wish she'd kept it to show to Dad because he might have been able to identify it, but it spooked her too much. She put a glass over it, and I had a look while she went to get a postcard to slide underneath the glass so that she could take it out into the garden. It really was the most horrific-looking creature I have ever seen. It was big – about an inch long – with kind of horny things growing out of it and a pattern like leopards' spots. Mama dumped it in the furthest corner of the garden by the composter.

'I wouldn't have thought it's a native species,' Dad is saying. 'It probably came into the country in a container of bananas or something. That's probably how that spider you terminated got into the country, too.'

'Holy *shit*!' Mama lets out a shriek and clutches Dad's arm. An enormous frog has landed inches from her bare foot.

'Another of my mother's familiars,' observes Dad, laconically.

Mama laughs and I do too because I know that witches' pets are called 'familiars'.

Dad gets to his feet and stretches. 'Come on, angel. We'd

better get her into a bath. And I know you're not going to
want to hear this, but you're going to have to get her dressed
in real-life clothes today.'

'Why?'

'I've been asked to write a piece on Asherley Gardens.
We're going to have to go down there so I can do a bit of
research. But look on the bright side . . . they've just opened
a rather good new restaurant in the Visitors' Centre, and
lunch is on Mum.'

12

LILIES THAT FESTER

Granny has been bathed and dressed and anointed with *Je Reviens*. I'm sitting with her in the Brown Study. She's having a fix of David Attenborough while Dad does online research about Asherley Gardens (it has a pet cemetery, according to the website) and Mama does the hoovering.

The *Planet Earth* theme tune comes to an end and David Attenborough's honey tones drip through the speakers. 'Oh, I *do* love his voice,' says Granny. 'Hasn't he a beautiful voice, Katia?'

I nod. David Attenborough really does have a lovely voice. I wish I had any kind of voice.

Granny turns her stony gaze on me. 'Do you like my trousers?' she asks.

I nod a polite assent.

'I got them in Scotland, I think. You should get yourself a pair.'

Granny's trousers are of some crease-resistant man-made material, stretch-waisted for comfort.

'I remember you when you were just a tiny baby, you know,' she says. 'I brought your mother smoked salmon. I

92

drove to the maternity hospital to visit her, and afterwards I had tea in the Hilton. I'm a very good driver, you know. I used to drive to Scotland all the time. I could get in my car and drive there now, if I wanted.' There's a pause, and then she adds, conversationally, 'Did I tell you about my giraffes?'

Giraffes? I shake my head.

'I looked out of the window the other day and there were two giraffes in the garden. The people in the house down the road own them and they came to visit me.'

Oh. She must mean the peacocks. What a weird thing dementia is! I wonder, does Granny really think she saw giraffes in the garden, or has she just got the wrong word for peacocks? I wonder what it would be like to read Granny's stream of consciousness, if she were able to write it down. It would probably make even more riveting reading than Terry Pratchett.

'I used to play golf in Scotland,' Granny says. 'Golf is a great sport. I used to be lady captain of the golf club, you know. There was golf on the television all week. I should have liked to have gone to watch it, but I had nobody to go with.'

Now she's got golf confused with cricket.

'I was nearly as good a golfer as I was a driver, you know, Katia. And I wasn't bad-looking. Quite the reverse, actually. I was an actress, once upon a time. I played Jane Eyre in the West End in the Albery – or was it the Phoenix? – and men used to queue up outside the stage door to meet me. That's how I met my husband. Maurice. Did he die, I wonder? I think he may have died, you know. He may have died in our holiday shack. Or he may have died in hospital. Anyway, wherever he died, he's dead now. A lot of my friends are dead, Katia. All the interesting ones. Sadly, the boring ones live longer but I couldn't be bothered with them. I was great friends back in the day with all kinds of writers and artists and bohemian types. When I was a very young woman, Lucian Freud painted a picture of me. I wanted my parents to buy it, but they said it wasn't a good likeness and far too expensive. I understand his paintings are worth a fortune now. I collected paintings once. I had a beauty that used to hang above the fireplace in my sitting-room. It's gone now: I don't know where.'

It was sold, to keep Granny here in her home. The holiday shack she had on the coast was sold too. It was falling down, but Dad just loved that place. We used to go there a lot in the summer. Lola came too sometimes, and we'd explore and go crabbing and feed carrots to the donkeys: we were told always to offer the carrot on the palm of our hands because otherwise you ran the risk of being bitten. Dad maintained the place as well as he was able – he'd plant trees and repair fences and paint gates – but in the end it took too much time and money to keep it going.

'Lucian did a little doodle in my autograph book, I remember. And so did his brother, Clement. Alec Guinness and Deborah Kerr signed it, too, and David Niven. David was a complete charmer. He used to give the most amusing parties.'

I've never heard of David Niven or Deborah Kerr, but I know Alec Guinness was Obi-Wan Kenobi.

'And the Kray twins signed it.' The *Kray* twins? Mama saw a documentary about them recently. They were the most notorious gangsters in London back in the 1960s. I wonder what Granny was doing hanging out with *them*?

'And Dirk Bogarde. I met him at a film premiere. He was charming – but far too young for me. And I think he may have been homosexual. Not that I have anything against homosexuals, but *nul points* for him as far as we ladies were concerned. I think you call homosexuals "gay" now, don't you? I think that's rotten – *rotten* – that the word "gay" has been taken over and made to mean something that it doesn't. I like to say that I'm in a "gay" mood or such and such, or that I'm singing a "gay" song, but nowadays I suppose people would laugh at me if I said such a thing. It may be quite valuable now, Katia, that autograph book. Maybe you could sell it to buy some toys.'

Toys! Granny obviously thinks I'm still a little kid.

It's funny, isn't it, how I never imagined Granny having a life – gay or otherwise – before she became Granny? I'd known that she had been an actress, of course, but only in a vague way. You just don't bother, do you, to find out about people you take for granted, like grannies and grandpas – or even mothers and fathers? You don't really think that grown-ups could have led interesting lives of their own. I wonder how much else I don't know about Granny, and if this is just the tip of the iceberg, like the one David Attenborough's been talking about for the past five minutes.

'When I was lady captain of the golf club—'

No! I'm off. I don't want to hear about golf.

In the sitting-room, Mama and Dad are having an argument about her laptop.

'It's driving me mad,' she says. 'It's taking forever to get online.'

'It's because the connection here is slower than at home, Tess,' says Dad patiently.

'Whatever. Anyway, I'm fed up with it.'

'I'll install your updates for you and clean up your cache. That should make things faster for you.'

'The bloody thing has a mind of its own. It keeps ordering me to install things I'm not remotely interested in.'

'You really should install updates when it tells you. Because otherwise you're asking to be hacked. You'll start getting malware and trojans and . . .'

Pah! Dad's talking computer nerd talk. I think I'd rather hear Granny reminisce about her days as lady captain.

I wander back into the Brown Study and have a look at the bookshelves that line the walls. There's *Anna Karenina*, *Madame Bovary* and *Wuthering Heights*. *The Love Songs of Petrarch*. An *Encyclopaedia of Gardening*, the *Oxford Book of English Verse*, the *Complete Works of Shakespeare*. There are dozens of biographies of film stars of yesteryear. There's *Jane Eyre* . . .

These are books that Granny used to read and love – you can tell by the creases on the spines. I picture Granny in her young and beautiful days, maybe sitting under a tree by a river, with one of her beaux reading Petrarch to her, or one of Shakespeare's sonnets. I wrote an essay once about a Shakespearean sonnet that had the line, 'lilies that fester smell far worse than weeds.' They really do stink, you know, festering lilies. I remember this because any time Mama got Easter lilies, she never remembered to change the water and the pong was gross. But that's the point of the poem. Shakespeare is talking about what happens when youth and beauty fades.

Granny in her young and beautiful days is looking right back at me, because one of the shelves is devoted to family photographs. There are a fair few photos of Granny's parents; it's funny to think that she believes them to be alive still because those photographs are so old that *nobody* in them could possibly be alive. Apart from Granny, of course.

There are lots of photos of Dad and my aunt Gemma, and several of me as a baby, and as a toddler.

'You came to stay with me once, when you were just a toddler, you know.' It's as if she's read my mind! 'I think you were around two, or maybe a little bit older. Your parents had to go off to a funeral somewhere and couldn't take you with them.'

I guess it would have been to organise my other grandma's funeral. Mama told me that after Grandma died, she often rang her empty house in the vain hope that she'd got it wrong and that her mother would answer. It would be nice to think that one day in the future someone might invent a telephone that could put you in touch with your dead loved ones. Of course, Granny seems to think that it's already been invented.

'We had such fun that time, Katia!' Granny is saying. 'You were the prettiest thing, with a head of golden curls like a miniature film star. Like Kim Novak. I remember I organised a picnic in the garden for us, and I gave you all kinds of treats that your mother would never have dreamed of allowing you – like Turkish Delight and fudge and fizzy orange. I know it was naughty of me to give you sweeties, but I so wanted you to love me. I was scared that you might think I was some witchy old crosspatch – I didn't get to see that much of you, you see, because of living out here in the country. And that day we spread a rug on the lawn and scattered it with daisies and played pat-a-cake pat-a-cake baker's man, and you kept saying "Laugh, Granny!" and I did laugh, you know. I laughed a lot during those few days when I had you all to myself. I think it was out of pure joy – I never knew that one could feel so brimful of love for a child that wasn't one's own. And I felt very proud indeed that you had inherited my nose. Such a pretty nose we have, don't we, sweetheart?'

Granny's smiling – really smiling! The mouth that is usually all turned down at the corners in marionette lines is actually curved upward. I haven't seen her smile like that in years.

'Do you know, I just love it when I get little memories like this. It's like a treat. I remember I used to sing you to sleep – even though I was never much of a one for holding a tune. I knew even then that you were a very special little girl. I loved talking to you – still do, of course!'

I return the smile. Of course Granny loves talking to me because I listen to her. I mean, proper listening – not just going through the motions the way Mama and Dad do. They answer her on automatic pilot – especially Dad, when he's driving. You'll see what I mean when we head off to Asherley Gardens.

'How's David Attenborough, Mum?'

Dad has poked his head around the study door.

'Who's that?'

'It's Donn, Mum. Your son.'

'Oh, yes. What do you want?'

'I was wondering how you were getting on with David Attenborough – on the telly.'

'Oh – is that who that is? I haven't been listening to him. I've been having a nice chat with Katia.'

I smile at Granny, then turn back to Dad, but he's gone.

A couple of minutes later, Mama comes into the room.

'We're going to head off to Asherley Gardens soon, Eleanor. Would you like to spend a penny before we go?'

'Oh, no. I don't think I can be bothered.'

'I think it's probably not a bad idea actually, Eleanor.

There's a new restaurant there, and I don't know where the loos are.'

'Don't they have loos?'

'Oh, I'm sure they do. But it's probably a better idea to spend a penny here first. It means we don't have to go hunting around for them in the restaurant.'

Mama's voice is strained. I know she's anxious for Granny to do a wee before we go because she's terrified that she might have an 'accident' in the restaurant, like she did in her slippers the other day. She was teetering along the corridor behind Mama and all at once she stopped and just peed straight there and then, without seeming to notice or care.

Granny looks mutinous for a moment, then relents. 'Oh, very well, then,' she says. 'I suppose I must do as I'm told.'

'Come on, then.'

Mama reaches for Granny's hands, to pull her to her feet. 'Oh! Your hands are like stones!'

'Yes. I have poor circulation.'

'What?'

'I said I have poor circulation.'

'You're an awful mumbler, you know.'

'Yes! I am!' shouts Mama.

'There's no need to shout.'

Mama raises her eyes to heaven in exasperation.

'Where do you want me to go?' asks Granny.

'To the bathroom. To spend a penny. Follow me.'

Granny leaves the room and I hear her stumping down the corridor. On the telly, David Attenborough is talking about global warming and climate change – and it's all down to us. 'Humankind' is a contradiction in terms. Humans are not kind. We've raped the planet and pillaged and plundered it, and it serves us all right if we die from rising sea levels or freak storms or tornadoes. We are not meek, and we don't deserve to inherit the earth. Let everything disappear back under the sea where we came from. That's where we belong. Except we don't deserve the world under the sea, either. It's way too beautiful down there.

A voice floats the length of the L-shaped corridor. It's not the kind of voice you'd expect from a ninety-year-old. It's not quavery or piteous or apologetic. It's rather a strident voice, peremptory, a voice that's used to issuing commands and having them obeyed. 'I need help! *I need someone to help me!*'

'What's the problem, Eleanor?' Mama passes the door, on her way back to the bathroom.

'I need someone to help me pull up my pants.'

'Coming, Eleanor,' says Mama.

13

PET CEMETERY

We're off on our jolly – our outing to Asherley Gardens!

Granny's sitting in the front of the car beside Dad, and I'm in the back with Mama, with my head on her shoulder. I made Mama a collage of photographs once for her birthday, of her and me and Dad and our cat, who's dead now, and in loads of the photographs that's just the way we are – me sitting beside Mama with my head on her shoulder, and her with an arm around me.

Being in the back of the car means that Granny's forgotten about us, so we don't have to join in the riveting conversation she's having with Dad, which goes like this:

'Where are we going now?'

'We're going to Asherley Gardens, Mum.'

'What for?'

'For lunch. We've booked a table.'

'Did you tell them the name?'

'Yes.'

'Because they'll know us, you know. They'll know the Ellis name. We're a very well-known family.'

'Yes, Mum.'

Granny starts to sing. '*S'wonderful. S'marvellous* . . .' Dad joins in for a few bars, even though he doesn't have a clue about the words, other than '*S'wonderful*' and '*S'marvellous*'.

Then: 'Where are we going now?' asks Granny.

'We're going to Asherley Gardens.'

'What for?'

'For lunch.'

'And where are we now?'

'We're on the motorway, heading south.'

'I don't care about all these people heading south. What's that?'

'It's a Post-It pad, Mum.'

'What's a Post-It pad?'

'It's a pad for jotting down notes. There's adhesive on each page so you can stick them on things.'

'Why?'

'As a memorandum. See? Like this.' Dad tears a page off the pad with his left hand and sticks it onto the dashboard.

'Oh. That's very ingenious, isn't it?'

'Yes.'

'*Was tün wir?*' Granny has a habit of talking in German sometimes, I don't know why. She has kind of catchphrases that she trots out: *Was ist das hier? Was hast du gesagt? Wo gehen wir?*

'Where are we going now?'

'We're going to Asherley Gardens, Mum.'

'And is there a purpose in going to these gardens?'

'Yes. We're going to have lunch.'

'Oh. Do you like my trousers?'

'Yes. They're very nice. They're herringbone, are they?'

'What?'

'I said "are they herringbone?"'

'I don't know what sort of bone they are. Dum de dum de dum de dum. *Little boxes. On the hillside.*'

'Yep. They're building little box-like houses all over the place.'

'But we don't *like* that, do we? Do we?'

'No. We don't.'

'*How much is that doggie in the window?*'

'Wuff wuff,' Dad goes, obligingly.

'I think I'll get a dog. I'm going to get a dog.'

'Yes. You've always loved dogs.'

A pause, then: 'Where are you actually heading for?' asks Granny.

'Asherley Gardens, Mum.'

'Are you going to stay there?'

'No. We're going for lunch. And I think we might pick up some eggs, will we?'

'Where will you get eggs?'

'From the Bainbridge's farm. They do lovely fresh free-range eggs. Fresh eggs – yum yum. Shall we listen to the radio?'

'No. I don't want the radio. Where did you say we were going?'

'Asherley Gardens.'

'Will we be able to get anything to eat there?'

'Yes. We're going for lunch.'

Where are we going now?

I guess it's like that refrain so beloved of very small children. *Are we there yet? Are we there yet? Are we there yet?* Except in Granny's case it's *Where are we going now?* You could record this pointless conversation and play it on a loop. I could copy and paste it, copy and paste it, copy and paste it. Although Granny does occasionally come out with some classics, and today these include 'I love not knowing where I am' and, on our arrival at the gardens, 'This is a lovely place! I'm going to buy this place.'

Getting Granny out of the car takes forever, and she gives out yards. Then, between us, we manoeuvre her through the car park and into the restaurant. It's crowded, and you can see people exchange glances that say, quite clearly, *Oh my god, I hope that old bat's not going to be seated at the table next to us . . .*

I feel like standing up on a table and making a speech about the ageing demographic, and how everyone'll be like this one day. And, hey – at least we're doing our bit, relieving Granny of a little of her humdrum housebound existence by taking her out for a jolly.

There are some other pretty ancient people here, too, having lunch: mostly mothers with women who are clearly their daughters; you can tell by the physical resemblance. Somebody famous made a joke about how tragic it was that all women turn into their mothers, and how even more tragic that no men turn into theirs. But what if . . . What if Dad turned into Granny? What would Mama do then? Would she have to wipe his bum and singalong-a-nursery-rhyme and resign herself to taking abuse from him?

I wonder is Mama turning into *her* mother? Mama's mother – who I called Grandma to differentiate her from Granny – had cancer. I was two and a bit when she died, but it wasn't the cancer that killed her. She took her own life when she discovered the cancer was terminal. She really, really didn't want to die in hospital, you see; she wanted to die in her own home surrounded by flowers and with Mozart on the CD player.

I found out about this just before my thirteenth birthday,

when my dad was writing an article for his paper on something called Voluntary Euthanasia. He had a letter on the desk in front of him when he was writing the article: it was the letter Grandma had written to her family just before she died. I asked if I could read it, and he said yes, that he supposed I was old enough now to know about things like that.

Anyway, Grandma's letter was beautiful. She'd written it just before she'd taken the pills. She'd been everywhere and done everything she'd ever wanted, she said, and when I asked Mama if that was true, she said yes – that Grandma had been a free spirit who had spent the last summer of her life living on an island on one of the Canadian Great Lakes, skinny-dipping every day. I suppose she was a kind of hippy, my grandma, compared to Granny. Granny is – or was . . . *refined*.

I guess that maybe Mama *is* turning into her mother, because there's something a bit hippy-ish about her. I used to be embarrassed sometimes when she picked me up from school because she'd be wearing different kinds of clothes to most of the Yummy Mummies – wifty wafty boho things: harem pants and dangly earrings and quirky vintage pieces. Working as a 'creative' in advertising means that a little eccentricity is expected, you see.

We ask for menus, and Granny comes out with stuff like 'What does that funny-looking person think he's doing?' (he's the manager) and 'Who's that silly old bitch over there?' (she's a fellow diner). And she makes these remarks in really quite a loud voice, so lunch is pretty excruciating. And when the waiter comes to take our order, Granny peers at him and says, 'How do you do . . . Long John Silver?' And of course, Mama has to constantly remind Granny that the drink in the tumbler to her right is elderflower pressé, and the food on the plate in front of her is fish pie, and Granny insists that she ordered crab salad like Dad, not fish pie, and her nose runs and she blows it and sets her handkerchief on her side plate, and I see Mama cringe.

At the next table, two girls are sitting side by side, studying a glossy magazine. It's a special issue on how to 'Work the Trends from Seventeen to Seventy Plus', and it's full of famous older women.

'Oh my god – look at her!' says one of the girls. 'She's *never* in her sixties! Ooh, look – she's wearing Christian Louboutins! I'd love to think that I could look that good when I hit her age. I wonder how she pulls it off?'

I slide them a disdainful look. It's a no-brainer, isn't it? These dames keep themselves looking like this because they can afford to spend a fortune on facial peels and cosmetic surgery and designer clothes. I picture Granny's bunion-bedecked feet crammed into Louboutin heels, then stifle a giggle.

'And this old doll's *eighty*!' gasps the other girl. 'It's really great to think that women still make an effort to look that good when they're so, like, past it, isn't it?'

Is it? I wonder. Over by the window a woman is picking at a green salad. She is shockingly thin, with jutting collar- and cheekbones; the tendons in her neck are stretched and stringy, and her skinny fingers seem to droop under the weight of her bejewelled rings. Her skin is pulled tight over her face like Lycra, and her lips are so swollen it looks as though she is suffering from anaphylactic shock. She's probably in her seventies.

She's made an effort. She's worked hard to keep her figure 'girlish' and she's gone under the knife to keep her

106

skin wrinkle free, but she still looks as shocking as Granny –
although in a different way.

Mama told me that most of those film stars in the books
on Granny's shelves ended up washed up and caved in and
burned out: used and abused by the studios and by the
men they were dumb enough to marry, staggering through
middle-to-old age on a pills-and-alcohol combo, trying to
cling on to youth and beauty and all looking like parodies of
themselves at the end. None of them lived to a ripe old age.

Ripe old age. As if! There's nothing ripe about old age: it's
all dry and wizened and wasted. If you had the bottle to read
my description on page forty-nine, you'll know that already.

I wonder if Granny had gone to Pinewood Studios,
would she have ended up driven to drink and despair by the
ruination of her beauty? Mama tried her best with Granny
today, she really did. She put some pancake foundation and
powder on her face, and made sure there was no lipstick on
her teeth, and chose her outfit with care. Granny's wearing a
fawn cashmere sweater (to match her fawn and tan trousers),
a string of pearls, and brown faux-suede shoes that stretch
to accommodate her bunion. But I could tell by the sidelong
looks that those gals at the next-door table exchanged when
they saw her shuffle in earlier that they were, like, completely
freaked by her appearance.

Dad's excusing himself, getting up from the table, heading
off out to do his research on Asherley Gardens. Granny's
oblivious, engrossed in the coffee cake she's eating. She
sucks loudly on her fingers after each bite, and Mama's
staring out the window, and I know she's wishing she could
put her hands over her ears and hum something uptempo. I
decide to go with Dad, and throw Mama a 'Sorry!' look as I
follow him through the restaurant. She'll understand. She'll

know I want to spend time alone with him over the weekend.

We trail along woodland paths, Dad and I, and through leafy tunnels, breathing in that lovely odour of damp earth mixed with unidentifiable plant smells and the rushy ozone of the river. Dad's absorbed, making notes, so I wander hither and yon, wishing I had a camera. I won't even bother to describe the beauty of the place: I don't have the words for it. That's Dad's job.

I catch up with him as he stops to read the names on the headstones in the pet cemetery. *Top Dog Muffin. Darling Scampi. Dear Toppi. Precious Jolly.* There are tears in his eyes, and I wonder, is he thinking about our cat, Batty Thomas, who died of kidney failure?

I lay a hand on Dad's arm. I hate to see him look sad. I hate to see him look his age. My mama and my dad were a stunning couple once, but now they have that kind of defeated, resigned-to-being-a-loser look to them. Life's knocked them about – them and loads of their baby-boomer friends – and it shows.

They don't see as many of their baby-boomer friends as they used to. They can't afford to go out much. Mama and Dad and their friends used to talk about selling up and heading off to live the Good Life in a village in the South of France or Tuscany or the West of Ireland, but everyone has too many commitments: kids who need to be educated, mortgages that need paying off, ageing parents who need to be cared for. The so-called baby-boomer generation is stuck between a rock and a hard place; between the Gap Year and the Nursing Home; between penury and pension plans.

I remember my parents in the days when they had a bit of money to splash around. They used to invite people to dinner, and have barbecues and kitchen suppers and poker sessions and Murder Mystery parties and birthday parties and fancy-dress parties and parties for no reason at all. Just to celebrate the fact that life was good. Lola and I used to dress up in black outfits to be maids sometimes, and a hat would be passed around for us, and inevitably guests would be lavish because they'd had too much to drink. There was so much laughter in those days! We had a crowd of friends to stay at the shack on the coast one hot, hot summer and laughter used to just bounce around the bay, ricocheting off the water and ringing round the dunes. And Mama and Dad were so much younger then, and looked so radiant. I think laughter is more beautifying than any cosmetic surgery.

They don't laugh at all now – except at their gallows humour jokes, and I'm not sure that the laughter that gallows humour provokes is very beautifying. Mama and Dad have lost all their radiance.

I look at Dad's miserable face as he stares at the pet cemetery, and then I shoot a meaningful look in the direction of the restaurant. Mama's been there on her own with Granny for too long now. It's not fair. It's time to rescue her and go back to the Gingerbread House.

14

A Grasshopper Walks Into a Bar

We're back. Granny is singing 'Congratulations and Celebrations' because Dad has successfully backed the car through the gate. Although she did say rather snittily earlier that if she'd been the one who was driving we would have been home by now.

'This is my house,' Granny announces, proudly. I think it's not so much that she's proud of the house as she's proud of the fact that she's actually managed to recognise it.

'Yes. This is your house,' agrees Dad.

'Will we get out now?' she asks.

'No. Let's stay in the car,' says Dad, sarcastically. I can tell by his tone that he's tired.

'I love this car,' says Granny. 'I love being here with you.'

Our car used to be quite posh: it's a Mercedes. But it's clapped out now, and the engine's making a funny noise. That'll be the next thing that will happen: the car will lie down and die and Dad'll have to get a loan for a new one, and that'll add another line to the downward-turning ones around his mouth and another grey strand to his thinning hair.

Once we've unloaded Granny and put her in the Brown Study, Dad goes back to Mama's computer to carry on cleaning it up. Her Skype's been acting up, too; sometimes when friends Skype her they say she goes all pixillated.

'Why don't you get in touch with them on Facebook?' he suggests.

'Facebook scares me.'

'It *scares* you? Why?'

'Because everybody on Facebook is so fucking happy. Look.'

She whisks us off to Facebookland with a click of her mouse and scrolls down to: Happy holidays. New handbags. Birthday celebrations. Proud parents. Yoga show-offs. Then the cursor hits on some video footage of divers doing backward rolls off an RIB.

'No,' says Mama abruptly, getting up from the table and leaving the room.

In the kitchen, I hear the sound of a cork being pulled. Dad glances at me and I pretend to look unfazed, concentrating on the images of divers doing BWRAF. Scuba diving uses really clumsy acronyms. There are literally hundreds – including my favourites: VENTID (for Vision Ears Nausea Twitching Irritation Dizziness) and BFK (Big Fucking Knife).

Dad skims the touch pad with his forefingers, and hits on this:

Win4Fiction Debut Playwriting Competition
    The Win4Fiction Prize for Playwriting has been respon-
sible for launching and furthering the careers of numerous promising playwrights. See more at: www.win4fic-
tion.co.uk

The prize turns out to be a copy of *The Ultimate Playwrights' Companion* by someone you've never heard of. But as Dad keystrokes and mouse clicks, I see that there are numerous playwriting opportunities out there on the worldwide web, including competitions for plays by and for young adults. Perhaps I could submit one?

Beyond the hatch, I hear the ping of the microwave. Mama must be defrosting tonight's dinner.

DINNER WITH GRANNY
A ONE-ACT PLAY BY KATIA ELLIS

Sitting on three sides of an old-fashioned mahogany dining table are GRANNY, KATIA *and* DONN. GRANNY *is sitting centre, with* KATIA *on her left and* DONN *on her right. The table is set with place mats, silverware, condiments and glasses. Two of the glasses contain wine. A sideboard stage left boasts a big vase of silk flowers. They are a bit dusty.*

DONN: The weather seems to have got a little cooler.

GRANNY: Cooler, cooler West Coast Cooler.

DONN: That could be a bit of a relief, actually. It was almost too hot in Asherley today.

GRANNY: Would you say it was unseasonably hot?

DONN: Unseasonably hot. Yes. That's a very good way to describe it.

TESS: (*enters with a tray*) Well! Here we are now!

DONN: (*rubbing his hands together in exaggerated enthusiasm*) Excellent! Grub's up, Mum!

GRANNY: What are we having?

DONN: Looks like shepherd's pie to me.

TESS: Yes! It is shepherd's pie!

DONN: Made by your own fair hands, no doubt? Ha ha ha.

TESS: Ha ha ha. No. It is Tesco's finest.

TESS *puts the tray down on the sideboard and starts to set plates on the table.*

GRANNY: What is it?

112

DONN: It's shepherd's pie, Mum.

GRANNY: Oh, good. I love shepherd's pie.

DONN: We all love shepherd's pie.

> TESS *takes a seat between* KATIA *and* GRANNY.

DONN: (*taking up a fork*) Mmm, it is delicious.

TESS: Tesco's finest. Every little helps. We really care about our customers.

GRANNY: What's that you're saying?

TESS: I'm saying that Tesco's really care about their customers. They go to extraordinary lengths to keep them satisfied. Everything they stock is hand-picked and lovingly packaged. To save the customers precious time, they pick it, trim it, wash it, mix it and pack it themselves.

GRANNY: What a lot of rubbish you're talking.

TESS: Yes. Rubbish is exactly what I'm talking.

> TESS, DONN *and* KATIA *smile at each other. Then* TESS *and* DONN *pick up their wine glasses, raise them in a toast, and swig.* GRANNY *takes up a fork and peers at her plate.*

GRANNY: What is it?

DONN: It's shepherd's pie, Mum.

GRANNY: I'm going to eat this now. Shall I eat it?

DONN: Yes. Do.

> GRANNY *dips her fork into the pie and manages to scoop some up. As she brings the fork to her mouth, a lump of mashed potato drops on to her lap.*

TESS: Oops. I'll get a cloth.

GRANNY: I don't have a napkin! Why don't I have a napkin? I should have a napkin.

TESS: I'll bring you one now.

> TESS *gets up and leaves the room. She returns with a cloth and some linen napkins, wipes mashed potato off* GRANNY'S *lap, then distributes the napkins.*

113

TESS: Nappies for everyone.

DONN: In your dreams.

TESS, DONN *and* KATIA *try to stifle their laughter.*

GRANNY: What's so funny?

DONN: Nothing. I just remembered a joke.

GRANNY: Well, if it's so side-splittingly funny, I think you might have the manners to share it.

DONN: Um. OK. A grasshopper walks into a bar . . .

TESS: Thank god! A joke!

DONN *smiles at* TESS *and takes her hand.*

DONN: A grasshopper walks into a bar. The barman looks astonished. 'Hey, whaddaya know?' he says. 'We have a cocktail named after you.' The grasshopper gives him a bemused look and says, 'You have a cocktail called Steve?'

DONN *and* TESS *laugh out loud. It is clear that neither* KATIA *nor* GRANNY *has understood the joke.*

GRANNY: (*frostily*) I don't think that's remotely amusing.

DONN: (*with a sigh*) Well, there's a cocktail called a grasshopper, you see. Made with Crème de Menthe and Crème de Cacao. But the grasshopper's name is Steve.

KATIA *smiles, but* GRANNY *remains stony-faced.*

GRANNY: I think that is not a joke at all. Or if it is, it's a very silly joke. You should be ashamed of yourself, telling such silly jokes. What age are you now?

DONN: I'm forty-eight, Mum.

GRANNY: You're never forty-eight!

DONN: I sure am. And feeling every day of it.

GRANNY: But are you my son?

DONN: Yes.

GRANNY: Then what age am I?

DONN: You're eighty-nine, Mum.

GRANNY: But I don't want to be eighty!

DONN: You're not eighty, Mum. You're eighty-nine.

GRANNY: But that's a dreadful age!

DONN: Yes.

GRANNY: I'm carrying on the tradition of my family. Living to a funny old age. My parents are still alive, you know. Aren't they?

DONN: What do you think, Mum?

GRANNY: No. It's terrible when your memory deserts you.

DONN: (*with a shrug*) That's what happens when you reach eighty-nine. It's OK. It's not your fault.

GRANNY: Am I eighty-nine? Oh – that's far too old. I should have popped my clogs by now. I don't want to be eighty-nine. Little old ladies are meant to be sweet and wrinkly and loveable. I'm a horrible person. I've turned into a horrible person. Why am I such a horrible person?

DONN *and* TESS *exchange glances. They eat in silence for a while.*

GRANNY: (*looking at* DONN) Did you marry someone?

DONN: Yes, I married Tess.

GRANNY: Tess? (*looking at* TESS) Is that you?

TESS: Yes, Eleanor.

DONN: My faithful, unselfish, long-suffering wife.

GRANNY: Oh, I wouldn't believe that for a moment!

DONN: Take it easy, now. Don't say anything if you can't say something nice.

GRANNY: All women are selfish. If you don't know that, you know nothing, and you're stupider than you look.

DONN: Mum, I don't want to have a row here.

TESS: (*laying a hand on* DONN'S *arm*) It's OK. This is interesting.

GRANNY: Why are you whispering? You don't want me to hear!

DONN: (*loudly*) We're not whispering, Mum.

TESS: Do you think I'm selfish, Eleanor?

GRANNY: (*autocratically*) You have your moments, I'm sure.

KATIA *gives* GRANNY *an indignant look.*

TESS: Are you selfish, Eleanor?

115

GRANNY: (*with a brusque laugh*) Oh, that's for sure!

TESS *and* DONN *exchange glances.*

GRANNY: Stop giving each other private smiles. It's rude.

DONN: But we're married. We're allowed to smile at each other. (*lowering his voice*) And do rude things.

GRANNY: What do you mean you're married?

DONN: Tess and I married each other quite some time ago.

GRANNY: Why did nobody *tell* me? I don't *believe* that the pair of you are married! Congratulations and Jubilations! (*to* TESS) Have you ever been in this house before?

TESS: Yes, I have.

GRANNY: Someone once called it the Gingerbread House, you know. I thought that was a delightful name to call it! It's such a pretty house, isn't it?

TESS: Yes. (*there is a pause, then she rises and starts to clear away plates*) I think I'll clear away now. Would you like a bowl of ice cream for pudding, Eleanor?

GRANNY: No. I would not like a great big bowl. I would like a dish of ice cream for pudding. Thank you.

TESS: You're welcome. (*exit*)

DONN: Well, that was lovely, wasn't it?

GRANNY: What did we have, again?

DONN: Shepherd's pie. Tesco's finest. Tesco's really care about their customers. They go to extraordinary lengths to keep them satisfied. Everything they stock is hand-picked and lovingly packaged. To save the customers precious time, they pick it, trim it, wash it, mix it and pack it themselves.

GRANNY: You talk an awful lot of rubbish sometimes, you know.

KATIA *and* DONN *smile. From the kitchen comes the sound of a plate smashing.*

CURTAIN.

116

15

SIGN OF THE FISHES

It's Sunday evening. Dad's just driven away from the Gingerbread House. We've waved him off and now Mama's trying to shut the gate.

'It could do with some DV8, or whatever that lubricant is,' she says. 'It's fucked. Everything in this house is starting to fall apart.' She gives a big sigh, then looks up at the sky. 'One week down, two to go. Let's go check out what scintillating stuff is on the telly this evening.'

In the Brown Study, *Appointment with Death* is coming to an end. It's the third time Granny has listened to it this week.

Mama helps herself to the television guide and sits down.

'*Was hast du gesagt?*' says Granny. 'What did you say?'

'Nothing, Eleanor. I'm just looking to see if there's anything on television.'

I look over Mama's shoulder as she scans the listings. *Embarrassing Bodies* is on. Granny could go on that.

'Hmm,' Mama says in an undertone. '*Sexy Cam*? *Pimp My Ride*? Or *Rude Tube*?'

'What are you muttering about?'

'I'm looking at the television page, Eleanor. There's a

programme on about elephants. Do you fancy watching it?'

'Would that be interesting?'

'It might be.'

'All right, then.'

The *Appointment with Death* music fades away.

'I'll just nip out and turn the dishwasher on,' says Mama, aiming the remote at the telly and leaving the room. She's got the wrong channel. It's MTV, and some muthafucka is rapping about slapping his bitches and hos, and there's a gang of bling girls in thongs and minuscule bikini tops gyrating around him.

Granny's stony eyes go to the television. She frowns, then leans forward. 'What's going on there?' she says. 'I can't see. What are they *saying*?'

I cover my mouth with my hand to hide my smile as Mama comes back into the room, lunging for the channel changer.

'Oh, it's just a pop video, Eleanor.'

'Keep it on. I like pop music. "Congratulations and Celebrations." That's Cliff Richard, you know.'

'Yes.' Mama zaps the telly. A close-up of an elephant's face comes on.

'I love Cliff Richard.'

'Yes.'

'Who's that?'

'It's an elephant.'

'What's it doing?'

'We'll soon find out.'

The camera pulls back to show us that it's mating with another elephant.

'Is it having sex?'

'Looks like it.'

'It's very overrated, you know. Sex.'

'Mmm.'

A man walks on to the screen. 'G'day,' he says jovially, and my heart sinks. He's Australian. Granny finds it difficult to understand any accent that isn't as posh as David Attenborough's. 'The elephants behind me have just finished rutting. This means that – if the rut has been successful – we can expect to see—'

'What's he saying? I can't make out a word. Turn it up.' Mama obliges, but it's a pointless exercise. '*What's he saying?*' shouts Granny again.

'He has an Australian accent, Eleanor,' says Mama.

'I don't have a clue what he's saying. Turn him off!'

'OK.' Mama's face is set. She tosses the channel changer onto a pouffe. 'Well. If you don't want to watch telly, maybe we should do the crossword instead.' She reaches for the Sunday paper and a Biro, and turns to the crossword page. Then she clears her throat, and says – very loud and clear – 'One across. "Old-fashioned rural roof covering." Six letters.' Mama writes THATCH along one across.

Granny thinks for a minute, then: 'Thatch,' she says.

'Yes. It must be thatch.' Mama moves on to two down. '"Suspend canine with shamefaced look."'

'What does that mean?'

Mama's writing HANGDOG along two down. 'I don't know,' she says. 'It's a tough one, isn't it? Let's go on to the next one.'

I see her run her Biro along the clues, clearly trying to find an easier one. She skips down to thirteen across. '"Old Nick. Satan."'

'Old who?'

'Old Nick, or Satan. Five letters.'

Granny thinks again.

'It might start with a D,' prompts Mama.

'Devil!' pronounces Granny triumphantly.

Mama writes DEVIL, then moves on to another clue. '"Sign of the fishes." Six letters.'

'What do they *mean* by "sign of the fishes"?'

'I think it might be a Zodiac sign, Eleanor.'

I know, I know! It's Pisces, my star sign!

'I had a car once called a Zodiac,' says Granny, proudly.

'What a lovely name for a car.'

'And I had a car coat to wear when I drove it, and driving gloves made of sheepskin.' Granny takes hold of the lapel of her fleecy gilet and squints at it. 'This is made of sheepskin. It's quite smart, isn't it?'

'Yes.'

Mama had helped Granny into it earlier, once the sun had gone off the garden. I wonder how she'll manage later, when she has to get her back into a nightgown. Operation Undress Granny takes some doing.

'"Lie back and relax",' says Mama.

'What? I'm perfectly relaxed, thank you very much.'

'No – it's a crossword clue. "Lie back and relax". Seven letters.' Mama writes RECLINE, and waits.

'I don't know what that is. Go on to the next one.'

'"A child's dog." Six letters.'

'Bow wow,' comes the immediate response.

'Yes!'

'*How much is that doggy in the window?*'

'Bow wow.'

Granny sings the song, and Mama dutifully bow-wows the responses, and then Granny says, 'I think I'll buy a dog. I used to have a dog. It was a miniature dachshund. They're

120

known as toy dogs, you know. *Two little boys had two little toys,*' sings Granny.

'Each had a something horse,' Mama adds automatically. She's been doodling in the Scribble Box. She's written my name over and over, in different kinds of writing. Katia. **Katia**. *Katia.* KATIA. *KATIA.*

I can't bear Singalong-a-Granny. It feels like the end of a long day. I'm going out, to the tree house. I'll talk to Charlotte or tell myself a story there, one of the hundreds that are stored in my head.

Alice was beginning to get very tired of sitting by her sister on the bank and of having nothing to do . . . when suddenly a White Rabbit with pink eyes ran close by her . . .

16

THE LIONS, THE WITCH AND HER WARDROBE

A bird caws. I look up to see a black crow squatting in the entrance to my osier pod. It looks almost as surprised to see me as I am to see it, and when I hoosh at it, it backs away and takes off to join its mate on the chimney of the Gingerbread House. The chimney has a ferny weed growing out of it.

I come down from the tree, then squeeze through the gap in the hedge into the garden. As I pass the study window, I see that Mama is standing in the middle of the room, staring at Granny with a freaked-out expression on her face. What's happened now?

In the study, Granny sounds as if she's been taken over by an alien. Except an alien might make more sense.

'Roug ge ug oh her wrds,' she says. 'Cuming cuming al rong out. Wat rite say. I no dont—'

'Eleanor, Eleanor – take it easy!' says Mama, hunkering down and taking Granny's hand.

Granny looks not so much unnerved as befuddled. 'Wrds al rite no rong. Al cum wardback. U no . . .'

'I know, I know. I'm listening. I'm trying to make sense of what you're saying.'

Granny's talking complete gobbledegook. But after I've listened for a few minutes, I kind of get the gist of what she's saying. It translates as:

'Happen me not right.'

'No. You're not right,' says Mama, trying to sound matter-of-fact. She's got quite good at that matter-of-fact tone over the course of the past week. 'But don't worry, Eleanor. I'm here to help.'

'I'm not right, you see. I'm looking for the right thing to do. I need to do the right thing. I'm stuck on the wrong side. I'm not *right*, you see.'

'I will help you find the right thing. I can try.'

'Will you tell me what to do?'

'I can't *tell* you what to do because this is your house.' Mama is using her best diplomat's voice. 'But I can suggest the right things you are looking for. Would that do? Maybe it's time to go to bed?'

'I am not right. I am telling you I am trying, I am trying to be right, and I'm not. I'm not making sense. I'm on the wrong side now and wroug ge uz oher wrds . . . Oh!' Granny's reverted to Alien. She clamps her hands over her mouth and gives a shaky laugh as she registers the absurdity of what's pouring out of her mouth.

'Well, if you're on the wrong side, we'll have to try getting you back on the right side, won't we?' Mama's trying to be upbeat, but she's scared too. I can tell by her eyes. 'Come on, Eleanor. I think you might need to lie down.'

Mama stands up and reaches out her hands, and Granny takes them. Things must be really bad because for once she doesn't tell Mama that her hands are like stones. And she's really unsteady on her feet as she passes into the hall, so Mama leads the way down the dark corridor with her arms out behind her, Granny clutching on, and it really is like something out of a zombie film: Granny's going qua qua qua, and when she gets into the bedroom she sits down heavily on the bed with her usual 'Oof!' and carries on about being on the wrong side and not being right, and then finishes up with 'I. Am. Dead.' I promise you that's what she says. And she really does look dead – white and exhausted and her eyes more unseeing than ever.

'Let's get you into your nightdress. And then we'll go and spend a penny.' Mama says 'spend a penny' now as easily as she used to say 'have a wee' or 'take a wazz'.

Very carefully, she eases Granny's arms out of her gilet. Then she removes the fawn cashmere jumper, and slowly manages to peel off Granny's herringbone trousers. They come away inside out, and Mama takes them outside into the garden to give them a shake because they're covered in flaky bits. I will never eat Crunchy Nut Cornflakes again. Vest and bra and knickers come next, and then Granny is shrouded in her nightdress, and Mama's helping her to her feet again and guiding her to the bathroom.

Mama's left the wardrobe door open. I wish I could step through into Narnia. But the back panel is solid, festooned here and there with the remains of cobwebs woven by Charlotte's ancestors. Inside, hanging alongside Granny's more everyday clothes are the smart ones she gets dressed up in for special occasions, like birthdays and Christmas. There's a glimmery silk dress, and a velvet skirt with a matching tunic, and an embroidered Chinese-style jacket. I remember she wore that to a family gathering once. She was sitting beside my aunt Gemma at the dinner table, and Mama was chatting animatedly to my uncle. Granny must have been jealous because I distinctly heard her say, 'Wouldn't you just love to *spit* at her.' I think that was the first time I was shocked by Granny.

Not long after that she described the newsreader on telly as a 'stupid fucking bitch'. That was the first time I heard her say 'fuck'. It was not the bad language so much as the pure nastiness in her tone; it was as if she was so full of such toxic hatred that it had to find a vent somehow. And I think that one of the reasons she was so full of hatred then was that she knew somewhere deep inside that she was no longer beautiful or witty or desirable; she couldn't get her head around that. So she wanted to knock other people and make them as wretched as she was.

On one of the many websites that Mama consulted before we came out here to the Gingerbread House, I read the following:

People with dementia can behave aggressively in one or more of the following ways:
   Being verbally abusive or threatening.
   Being physically threatening, such as kicking or pinching.
   Lashing out violently at people or property.
Try not to take it personally.

So far we've been lucky. There was the swipe with the face cream and the hair-pulling incident, but the idea that Granny might be capable of something more savage is making me jumpy.

They're coming back into the bedroom. Mama clears all the toy lions off the bed and pulls back the duvet so that Granny can sit down on the mattress. Then she lies back and Mama

125

lifts her legs and levers them onto the bed before tucking her in.

Don't forget the Aricept, Mama! I point to the bubble pack of pills and the tumbler of water on Granny's bedside table.

'Oops! I nearly forgot your pill, Eleanor,' says Mama. 'Sit up a little for me and I'll give you some water to help it down.'

'Why do I need a pill?'

'Because if you don't take it, you get cranky.'

'Crank*ier*, you mean,' says Granny, and we both smile at her little joke.

Mama puts the pill on the palm of her hand and Granny pokes about with her fingers until she finds it. I remember the rule about feeding donkeys. It makes me shiver to think that Granny might bite Mama. If she has her teeth in, that is. On a few occasions this week Mama has donned a disposable glove and snatched Granny's teeth from where she sometimes leaves them on the bedside table, so that she can take them into the bathroom and scrub them. When she does this, I notice that she keeps her eyes averted.

Mama holds the glass of water to Granny's lips, then sets it down on the table. 'I don't think we'll bother with a story tonight, will we?' she says, leaning down to give Granny a kiss on the forehead. 'You must be tired after talking all that fascinating gobbledegook!'

Granny manages a little laugh. 'Goodnight, love,' she says. 'Thank you.' And when I blow her a kiss from the doorway, she says, 'Goodnight, Katia.'

I know it's an awful thing to say, but I can't bear the idea of physical contact with Granny. Even the idea of kissing her on the forehead makes me go a bit queasy. And every time she holds out her hands for Mama to help her up from a chair or out of bed, I can't help wondering where those hands have been. I think Mama must have washed her own hands more this week than is good for them. It's just as well she got a tube of hand cream when she and Dad did their supermarket shop earlier on today. I noticed that there was Complan in the carrier bag, too. For Mama, not for Granny. Dad suggested it because Mama's not eating properly, even though Lotus warned her that she had to take care of herself.

The first thing Mama does when she gets back into the sitting-room is reactivate her computer and click on 'Favourites', and the second thing she does is Skype Dad. She's jabbering almost before Dad picks up, telling him all about Granny's 'turn'.

'I'm checking it out now,' says Mama. 'I've just gone to the online Family Doctor. Let's see . . . blah blah . . . Here we are. "Dementia: Warning Signs". Well, we know all about them. "Dementia: Caring for a loved one . . . Depression and Alzheimer's Disease . . . Facing loss: Death and—". Oh god, Donn. This is grim. This is grim.'

'Don't go there. Try Googling speech disorder. There may be something on that.'

Mama types in 'Speech Disorder' and waits. First up is Wikipedia.

I watch her scroll down a list. 'Blah blah . . . Cluttering, stuttering, apraxia, aphasia, dysarthria—'

'Click on dysarthria,' Dad tells her.

Mama scans the Wikipedia definition. 'Looks like this could be the one,' she says. '"Dysarthria can be an early symptom of stroke." Does that mean that she's *going* to have a stroke, or that she's already had one? Oh god, Donn. What if I go in there and find her dead in the bed?'

'Call me and I'll come straight out. You won't have to do anything.'

'Not close her eyes or anything, like they do in films?'

'No.'

Outside, a cat meowls. I catch a glimpse of a sleek dark body snaking under the gate, pursued by the red tom who lives two doors down. He leaps onto the pier of the gate to see off the trespasser, then turns and strolls nonchalantly on his way.

'By the way, Donn,' says Mama, 'the gate is rusting, and it's difficult to close. Can you bring some of that spray-on oil when you come at the weekend?'

'It needs repainting. I'll give George a ring and ask him to do it.'

'George has done his back in.'

'Oh, yeah. I forgot. His son, then. What's his name again?'

'Toby.'

Mama's abstractedly clicking the mouse as she speaks. From dysarthria on Wikipedia, her web browser has somehow transported her via TalkTalk and Carphone Warehouse to a yoga phone app. When she was made redundant, Mama did some research into becoming a yoga teacher. But training costs thousands, and she said that no matter how much practitioners insist that yoga is for all ages and all shapes and sizes, she'd never get a job because everyone wants their teacher to be fit and under forty.

But I'm glad Mama still practises. Some of the postures are really tough, so her muscles are steely. If she keeps it up it'll mean that she won't waste away like Granny, who can't even get up out of a chair by herself.

On a shelf in the sitting-room there is a golfing trophy that Granny won years ago. It's tarnished, and dirt has collected in the grooves and hollows. It shows a lady golfer teeing off, poised, willowy, perfectly balanced. Does Granny remember how it felt, I wonder, to be able to move like that, to have her body – sinews, spine, joints – under control, to swing her arms high, to perform a neat putt, to heft a bag of clubs over her shoulder and stride out across the fairway? Does she wonder, when her limbs don't do what her brain commands them to, what has happened to her own muscle and blood and bone?

On Skype, Mama's telling Dad she loves him. He says he loves her too, and then they end the call and Mama goes into the kitchen.

On the other side of the hatch, I hear the sound of a cork being pulled.

17

FEE FI FO FUM

'Hello, Katia. It's very early in the morning for you to come calling.'

'I couldn't sleep.'

'Are your other housemates sleeping?'

'Yes.'

'You've been here for over a week now. How are you today?'

'I'm not so good.'

'Would you like to tell me about it?'

'Mmm.'

'Why aren't you feeling good, Katia?'

'I didn't get much sleep last night.'

'Why was that, Katia?'

'Well, I lay awake for ages waiting for Mama to come to bed. And then, when she finally did come, I heard her stumble and fall outside in the corridor, and I didn't want her to know I was still awake so I just lay there in the dark until she came in. And then I heard Granny get out of bed and start stumping around the house, looking for people.'

'Who do you think Granny was looking for, Katia?'

'I think she might be looking for her children. Or else she's looking for dead people, like Maurice her husband, and her parents. She talks to them, you know. It really freaks Mama out when she does that. And you know, Charlotte, when Granny walks alone at night she seems to know exactly where she's going. She walks quite determinedly, and all you hear is stump stump stump. And I couldn't stop thinking of the giant in Jack the Giant Slayer, and the only words going round in my head were "Fee Fi Fo Fum", and they went round my head in the exact rhythm to Granny's stumping. And Mama had forgotten to lock our bedroom door, and I saw Granny poke her head round it, and it was just like in night vision – like you know when cameras can see people when the lights are all off? And I got dead freaked, and just lay there all stiff, pretending to be asleep. And then Granny went off and did some more stumping and muttering. And then it went quiet for a bit, but then the peacocks down the road started up their racket, and then it was dawn and the blackbirds started up their racket, and then I knew it was useless staying in bed any longer so I got up and went into the sitting-room. And Mama had left the light on and her computer was still on, and there was an empty bottle of wine on the table. And I looked at the web page that she'd been viewing before she went to bed last night.'

'What website had Tess been viewing, Katia?'

'Um. It was ... it was a forum for people who want to commit suicide. And it recommended loads of books. And at least one of the books gives instructions on how to do it. Everything from drowning to drugs.'

'That must have been very upsetting for you.'

'Yes. It was.'

'But Tess made a solemn promise to Donn, didn't she? That

she would ensure no harm came to Granny, and that she would do everything in her ability to see that Granny was well looked after. So she's not going to break her promise and do anything irresponsible while she is living here as her carer.'

'No. Mama never breaks her promises, but ... But I'm scared.'

'I can see how distressed you are, Katia. May I make a suggestion?'

'Yes, please.'

'Would you like me to sing to you?'

'Yes, please.'

'Which song would you like?'

'I'd like the song that Ariel sings in *The Little Mermaid*, please, Charlotte. "*Part of Your World*".'

'Wake up, Katia.'

'Did I fall asleep? Mama used to play that song to me as a lullaby. She told me that when she was pregnant she used to put the headphones on her tummy so I could listen too as I was floating around inside her. That means I've been listening to that music since before I was born. No wonder it sends me to sleep. Thank you, Charlotte, for going to the trouble of singing it to me. You have such a lovely sweet little voice.'

'And you have such lovely manners, Katia.'

'I learned them from Mama and Dad. They taught me that good manners make life easier, and to always look on the positive side of things. That's why it's so difficult for Mama living here, you see, because Granny's so negative about everything.'

'Why do you think that Granny is so negative about everything, Katia?'

'It's part of her disease.'

'Can you give me an example?'

'Well, it's like that time when Mama was watching the news and Granny started giving out yards about the couple whose little girl went missing and how it was all their own fault. She just can't seem to find anything nice to say about anyone or feel sympathy for anyone. And if you say something nice about a person, she always tries to twist it around and find something bad to say about them.'

'Why do you think Granny does this, Katia?'

'I think she's trying to show that she has opinions, too. I think that by arguing or saying something unpleasant when the person she's talking to is trying to be upbeat, she's trying to prove something.'

'What do you think Granny is trying to prove?'

'That she has her own identity still, that she has something valid to say maybe. And she works really hard at it, too. The other day, when Mama was pulling out a chair for her to sit at the dining table, she asked if the chair had a back to it. And Mama said, yes, of course. And then Granny realised that she ought to know that the chair had a back to it because it's her chair. And she thought and thought for a reply that would show this – you could see by her face that she was thinking really hard – and after a beat or two she went all kind of superior and said, "Because some chairs don't have backs to them, you know." As if Mama had been the stupid one all along. And I can see Mama droop more and more visibly when Granny pulls stunts like this, and I'm scared that she's not able for it. Granny's just chip-chip-chipping away at Mama's spirit. I read something on one of those dementia websites that said that it was important for carers not to wear themselves out, and how easy it was for this to happen, and for them to get depressed because of having to cope with all the aggression and disturbed nights and incontinence.'

'At least Tess hasn't had to cope with incontinence.'

'Apart from that time when Granny peed in her slippers.'

'Do you think Tess is depressed, Katia?'

'Yes. Wouldn't you be?'

'She's certainly going through a very tough time. But at least she is exercising regularly. They say that exercise helps lift feelings of depression. And once she starts taking her Complan she will feel stronger. Do you think she is working too hard at her book?'

'Yes. And you know she's writing about a child who's gone missing, and that can't help. I think she got the idea from all the stuff she's been watching on Sky News.'

'Perhaps that's why she was visiting websites about suicide, Katia.'

'What's that got to do with missing children?'

'Well, it wouldn't be unreasonable for a parent of a missing child to have suicidal thoughts. Maybe Tess has been doing online research for the new novel she's writing.'

'Do you know something, Charlotte? You could be right. When she was working as a copywriter she always used to buzz around weird sites on the internet, looking for ideas. It's all to do with lateral thinking.'

'In my opinion, Tess is simply researching her novel and there is no cause for undue concern.'

'Thank you, Charlotte. I *am* reassured. I always feel better after talking to you.'

'I am pleased to have been able to help.'

'Charlotte?'

'Yes, Katia?'

'Remember when you arranged for me to spend quality Dream Time with Mama so that I could talk to her?'

'Yes.'

'Could you arrange for me to do it again?'

'Katia, you know that in order for you to visit Tess, I will have to petition the Dream Spinner. The Dream Spinner gets many such requests. However, the Dream Spinner is aware of your special circumstances, and I have reason to believe that your request will be granted. Come to the Osier Pod before bedtime tomorrow evening and I will let you know the Dream Spinner's decision.'

'Thank you, Charlotte.'

'Have you anything in particular that you wish to communicate to Tess, Katia?'

'Not really.'

'Do you want her to tell you a story?'

'No. I want to tell her one. She needs a story more than I do.'

'You have a very generous spirit, Katia.'

'Thank you, Charlotte.'

'Goodbye, Katia. I look forward to talking to you in the Osier Pod again tomorrow.'

18

GROUNDHOG DAY

It looks like Mama's going to have one hell of a shiner. I reckon she hit her head off the blanket chest in the hall when she fell on her way to bed last night. I can tell by the way she won't meet my eye that she's embarrassed and doesn't want to talk about it: it's the elephant in the room.

Mama's day got off to the usual start when she brought Granny her cereal and welcomed her back to the land of the living dead by throwing open the curtains.

We've been lucky with the weather since we've been here and the forecast is for sunny spells to continue. It's just as well. Could you imagine if we'd had days and days of rain, and Mama hadn't been able to go for her run, or sit on the bench with the sun on her face, or take the phone out into the garden and pace up and down while she talks to her friends? She's been doing that a lot, talking to her gal pals. They've been a real lifeline: her only connection to the outside world.

But sometimes I don't think her forty-something friends quite understand. Some of them have small children and they seem to think that looking after a little old lady is a breeze in comparison.

'I'll swap you!' Suki said the other night. 'Running around after the twins is a nightmare!'

'At least you can just stick her in front of the television,' said Caitlin. 'I feel guilty if I'm not doing something creative with Flora, like finger-painting or baking.'

Or knitting a velociraptor, Mama could have added.

'Good morning, Eleanor. It's a beautiful day,' remarks Mama, cueing the dialogue that is reiterated every morning and that she now knows off by heart. It's true that it's a beautiful day: not even Granny could naysay that.

'Who is it?'

'It's Tess, Eleanor.'

'Oh, Tess! You're Tess . . . Sanders, aren't you?'

Sanders was Mama's maiden name.

'Yes, I am,' says Mama.

Granny blinks, as if she's trying to adjust her inkwell eyes to the light. 'Have you been in this house before?'

'Yes, I have.'

'What have you to do with our family?'

'I'm married to Donn, Eleanor.'

'Nobody ever told me Donn was married! I'm delighted. Welcome to our family.'

Granny's dysarthria, or whatever it was, seems to have been a one-off. Her enunciation is as crisp today as ever it was.

'Thank you,' says Mama. 'Now, here are your Crunchy Nut Cornflakes, with some chopped strawberries and a little cream, the way you like them.'

'Thank you. What day is it?'

Mama could pick any day at random. Monday, Wednesday, Saturday. Mother's Day, April Fool's Day, Groundhog Day. It's always the same day in the Gingerbread House.

137

'It's International Missing Children's Day,' she says.

'What did you say?'

'It's International Missing Children's Day. May 25th. It was on the news.'

'What a lot of rubbish you talk.'

'Yes.' Mama sets the bowl on the table and goes to get another pillow. 'I'll hoosh you up a bit, shall I?'

'I can hoosh myself up.'

But Granny does nothing. She just carries on lying there. All that stumping around in the middle of the night must have tired her out. I imagine David Attenborough doing a running commentary: 'While not normally prone to nocturnal activity, *Granis Granianus* occasionally emerges to check on the other inhabitants of the lair. It appears that her night vision is keener than her day vision because she certainly knows where she's going. She inspects the lair, chamber by chamber, before returning to her nest.'

Mama clears her throat. She's still hovering, with the pillow. 'If I hoosh you up, Eleanor, I can slide a pillow—'

'Oh, stop making such a fuss! I can hoosh myself up.'

Mama drops the pillow on the floor. 'OK,' she says.

'OK. *OK*. What's that supposed to mean?'

Mama doesn't respond. She just leaves the room, with her back very straight. She goes into the bedroom and emerges with her yoga mat. She's done the right thing. She's disengaged.

Granny lies on for a minute or two, then she pulls herself up so that she's lolling over the bed-table, and she starts to eat her Crunchy Nut Cornflakes. She's not hooshed up enough. Every time she brings the spoon to her mouth, milk dribbles onto the duvet cover. She dips the spoon in the bowl, drips, eats; dips, drips, eats, dips, drips, eats until all the Crunchy Nut Cornflakes are gone. Then she falls back against her pillows again.

In the sitting-room, Mama is doing Pranayama breathing. In the bedroom, Granny and me are also doing yoga. Granny is doing the Dead Body pose and I am doing the Pose of a Lion, which is when you open your eyes very wide and stick your tongue out as far as it will go. I know it's childish of me, but I just hate to see Mama being treated so shabbily, and pulling faces is the only way I have of making my feelings known. After I've bared my teeth and stretched my tongue and popped my eyes at Granny, I drift out into the garden.

I cocoon myself in my osier house, to think about happier times and holidays. We went to Malta once, on a dive holiday. The diving was nowhere near as gorgeous as Jamaica, and actually Mama hated Malta because when we went on a dive one day, Dad and I got lost.

It happened like this.

The dive sites of Malta are way overcrowded, you see. It's like conveyer belt diving, and every time our boat reached a site, there'd be a kind of competition amongst all the dive outfits to see who could get into the water first. You'd look around and see half-a-dozen or so dive boats with people on board all struggling to get their gear on, tugging on their wetsuits and performing giant strides into the water like lemmings. And on one of these dives Dad and I had buddied up and were messing about with his new underwater camera, and, to tell you the truth, we were being a bit careless because in scuba you must always, always keep an eye on the dive master leading the dive. So we finished taking pictures and carried on, but then realised that we were going in the wrong direction and had tagged on to a completely different group.

Mama told us afterwards that she had been finning along

behind the dive leader when she saw him look back to do a head count. And then the dive leader held up his hand the way a traffic cop does to say 'Stop!' And Mama saw him do a head count again, and she looked back and searched the water for me and Dad. It's really difficult to distinguish who's who underwater, what with all the masks and everybody dressed in the same rental gear, but something made Mama know with awful dread that it was me and Dad who were missing. And then the dive master aborted the dive by making the thumbs-up signal that means it's time to ascend, and Mama said that she finned up to the surface thinking that here she was, floating in the Mediterranean, a widow suddenly, who had lost her only child. And the group was all bobbing about, and the dive master was doing his head count again, and then me and Dad surfaced about a hundred metres away, feeling like right tools. And Mama gave out yards when we got back to the hotel: I have never seen her so angry. So we never went back to Malta, and I was glad, because actually the diving was pretty crap. Diving reefs in Jamaica spoils you for anywhere else in the world.

There's Mama now, heading off for her run. And – ooh! – there's Toby, strolling past the gate.

'Hi,' Mama says, running on the spot. 'Can I ask you a favour?'

'Sure,' says Toby with an easy smile, and I find myself wondering crossly if he's thinking that Mama's a MILF.

'I'm having a problem with the gate,' says Mama. 'It's getting difficult to close, and my husband suggested that I get it painted. Could you have a look and get back to me with an estimate?'

'Sure,' says Toby. 'When do you need the job done?'

'As soon as possible, I guess.'

'Well, I'm in college all week, and I can't do it this weekend because I've got something on. But I could do it the weekend after next, if that suits.'

'Fine.'

'I'll have a look at it now, and call in to you this evening with a quote.'

'Great. I'll make sure there's a beer in the fridge for you.'

'Cool. Thanks.'

'See you later, Toby.' And she's off, jogging along the tunnel of trees that lines the approach road to the Gingerbread House.

Hmm. He's eyeing her retreating rear. I think I've just gone off him.

Toby has a look at the gate from both inside and outside the garden. Then, as he turns to go on his way, I give a whistle, low and soft. He pauses, looks around. Ha! He's not sure he heard it or not. I whistle again, and from the look on his face I can tell he's a bit spooked. That'll teach him to look at my mama's ass!

Then the peacocks start up their din, and any chance of my whistling being heard is drowned out. Toby sets off up the road with a brief backward look over his shoulder, his green eyes narrowed against the sun.

I think of the little mermaid and her prince, and of how she could only express her love for him with her eyes. That's how I do it. That's how I express my love for Mama and Dad. They say that the eyes are the windows of the soul: but the little mermaid had no soul. They say that that's why mermaids so yearn to be transformed into humans, because it means they can be in possession of a soul.

I think being in possession of a soul is overrated. A bit – as Granny observed at dinner the other night – like sex. Don't

141

get me wrong! I have never had sex. I once went to a disco where loads of the girls took off their knickers before they went in, so that any boys they scored had access all areas. They just took off their knickers in full view of everyone in the queue on the road outside and stuffed them in their handbags. And all of them were wearing really, really short skirts and belly tops that skimmed their bras – even though not very many of them even needed bras, they were so young. And most of them were smoking, and loads of them were dead drunk, falling down and being sick all over the place. And one girl had passed out in a corner, and there were lads queuing up to do her.

I pretended to my friends that I was ill so that I could have a reason to call Mama and ask her to come and take me home. And in the car on the way back we talked about it, and Mama told me that having self-respect was way more important than trying to fit in.

I was different, even then. I guess I always have been different – 'a queer child, full of notions.' That's from E.B. White's famous book. It's how he describes Fern, his eight-year-old heroine, whose savviest friend is a kindly grey spider called Charlotte.

19

THE SELFISH GIANT

It's time for Granny's bedtime story. She's reclining against her pillows while Mama takes hold of her legs to lever them up onto the mattress. Mama's having problems, and Granny ends up lying in a funny position on her back, like a hieroglyph from the Ancient Egyptian *Book of the Dead*.

She's been in a tetchy mood for most of the day, so Mama just put her in front of David Attenborough and didn't try to engage at all. There are three hour-long programmes on each DVD, so the theme music repeats and repeats and repeats. I never want to hear the soundtrack to *Planet Earth* again ever in my life.

'I'm not terribly comfortable, you know,' says Granny, as Mama manoeuvres her legs around. 'It's always difficult to make yourself comfortable in an unfamiliar bed.'

'This *is* your bed, Eleanor,' says Mama.

'You mean this is the bed I slept in last night?'

'Yes. You're in your own bed, in your own bedroom, in your own house.'

'Is this my house?'

'Yes. Now. Here's your pill.'

'Why do I have to take a pill?'

'Because if you don't, you'll get cranky.'

'And I'm cranky enough, says you.'

'Ha ha. There you go. And here's a little water to wash it down. Now. How about your story?'

Granny brightens. 'Oh, yes, please! That'd be lovely.'

'"The Selfish Giant" by Oscar Wilde,' says Mama, opening the book at a page she's marked.

'The what giant?'

'The *selfish* giant.'

'Oh. All right. Go on.'

Oh, god. I hope Granny's not going to ask Mama to repeat herself every few words. That would try the patience of a saint, and Mama's been saintly enough today, IMHO. But as it happens, Mama makes sure to keep her decibel level up and her enunciation crisp, so that even Granny can have no complaints.

I stay to listen. I love the story about the giant who wouldn't let the children play in his garden, even though it has a very sad ending. Mama took me to see one of Oscar Wilde's plays once. It was called *Salomé*, and it was set in a royal palace in biblical times.

It was deadly boring.

The actor playing the king went on and on and on about all the treasures he'd heap on the princess, Salomé, if she did a kind of lap dance for him. For some reason I had a tennis ball in my backpack, and the ball had a slit in it. So I drew lips round the slit with a red felt tip, and then some eyes and a nose, so that when I squeezed the sides of the ball it could do emojis. And every time the king started droning on about his treasures and his peacocks and what have you, I manipulated the ball into all kinds of different facial

144

expressions. For example, when the king got really angry with Salomé his tennis ball face went all scowly. And when she did her dance he was all smiley. And when she asked him for the preacher's head on a plate he went totally apeshit with his mouth like OMG. And Mama and I started laughing – you know that agonising kind of laughter that you get in places like the head teacher's office when you're meant to be taking things really seriously? And we had tears spurting out of our eyes, and people were looking at us crossly because *Salomé* is a very artistic play. And then Mama snorted and someone went *Shh!*

We had to leave. We went along the row still choking with laughter and people had to stand up to let us pass, and when we got out into the foyer we just clung to each other and laughed and laughed and laughed.

Mama's coming to the end of the story now. She has tears of sadness in her eyes, and so does Granny.

'And the child smiled on the Giant,' says Mama, 'and said to him, "You let me play once in your garden, today you shall come with me to my garden, which is Paradise." And when the children ran in that afternoon, they found the Giant lying dead under the tree, all covered with white blossoms.'

'Oh!' cries Granny. 'That's very sad.'

'Yes,' says Mama, closing the book and setting it on the table. 'It is a sad story. But it's a very beautiful one. Goodnight, Eleanor. Sweet dreams. *Arrivederci.*'

I don't blow Granny my usual kiss because I get distracted. Someone's coming through the garden gate; I can tell by the clunk. I scoot down the corridor and peek around the corner. Beyond the glass door to the sun porch, I see Toby shut the gate behind him.

Mama's followed me. I look at her and make the scuba sign that tells her 'I don't wanna go there', shaking my head and passing my hands one across the other, palms foremost. I dive into the study, knowing it's highly unlikely that she'll invite him into its brown depths to enjoy a tinnie.

I'm right.

'Take a seat,' I hear Mama tell Toby. 'The bench under that window gets the last of the sun. I'll bring you out a beer.'

It's clever of Mama, to keep him outdoors. She'd be asking for trouble if she invited him into the sitting-room and Granny wandered in to find a strange man in her house. Although I suppose she's used to strangers. Every morning she wakes up to find me and Mama in her house, and she hasn't a clue who we are, how we got here, or what we're doing here. Every day Mama has to tell her that she's here because she's family, and what family does is look after each other. And some days Granny says that she doesn't need looking after and that she's perfectly capable of looking after herself, thank you very much.

Some days when she says this, I wonder what Granny would do if Mama said, 'Fair enough, I'll leave you to it.' What would she do if Mama and I walked out of the Gingerbread House and down to the village, got on the first bus back into the city and our home? *What would Granny do?*

What happens to people like Granny who have no one to care for them? Very often, when we used to take the byroads to the coast to go diving I'd sit in the back of the car and look along the overgrown driveways we'd pass, driveways that would lead to some low grey house (or 'dwelling') with tattered curtains and paint peeling off the door, and I'd wonder might there be someone living there, miles from

146

anywhere? Some old farmer, or some old farmer's widow? Or maybe there'd be a couple still, one looking after the other, trying to get by, the blind leading the blind.

I remember seeing a documentary once about some born-again preacher in America who was doing healing and he read out something from the Bible that said, 'The blind receive their sight, and the lame walk, the lepers are cleansed, and the deaf hear, the dead are raised up, and the poor have the gospel preached to them.' And it stuck in my head, for some reason – even though I am not a religious person. It stuck in my head because if all these cures are performed and if all these poor people have their bodily functions restored to them, what then? Their reward is to be *preached* to?

I think it's a bit like the politicians and the healthcare system. You make someone well by giving them a new hip or knee or whatever, and then send them home and expect them to get by on however many paltry effing quid a week. And then the poor people pay their television licence only to turn the telly on and have politicians preaching to them and hectoring each other.

I remember Dad going ballistic when he read in the paper about yet another expenses scandal. Apparently some MP went on the telly and told the taxpayers that they all had to tighten their belts and pay even more taxes because times were hard. And all the time this politician was living in a fancy house and eating in posh restaurants and buying fine wine and designer suits and holiday homes and expensive artwork and pagodas.

I look at the mark on the wall where one of Granny's paintings once hung and I wonder if politicians have to sell off any of their paintings or their homes to keep themselves in old age. Or if any of them have to fill out benefit forms

147

that make them cry. I saw that Mama had downloaded some PDF file to do with claiming benefits for carers; it was worse than scuba, with all the acronyms – CAB BEL ESA, etc.

That finishes this week's party political broadcast for the Gingerbread House Party. That's the Gingerbread House *Party*, not the Gingerbread *House* Party.

Thank you for listening.

20

THE GATEKEEPER

I hear the metal tab being pulled on a beer can. Mama and Toby are sitting on the bench outside the study window.

'Cheers,' says Toby. 'What happened to your eye?'

'I slipped in the shower,' lies Mama smoothly.

'Ouch. That's going to be a nasty one. Black eyes get worse before they get better.'

'I know. I'm just thanking my lucky stars that it wasn't worse. Imagine if I'd had to call an ambulance to take me to A&E? I'd have had to take Eleanor with me.'

'Who's Eleanor?'

'Mrs Ellis.'

'Why would you have to take her with you?'

'What else could I do with her? David Attenborough's only good for three episodes' worth of babysitting; I could have been stuck in A&E for the entire day.'

'David Attenborough?'

'Eleanor could watch him forever. Or listen to him, rather. When I need to get some work done, I put her in front of a box set. Although three hours is wishful thinking. Sometimes I might get forty minutes before she whistles for me to turn the volume up or find her handbag or bring her a cup of tea.'

'She whistles for you?'

'Let's not go there.'

There's silence for a couple of moments and then Toby says, 'Years ago they used to put a leech on a black eye, to suck the blood out.'

'Thank you for sharing that with me,' Mama says crisply. 'Shall we change the subject?'

'OK. How's your book coming along?'

'It isn't.'

'What's it about?'

'Don't want to jinx myself by talking about it.'

'So what are we going to talk about if we can't talk about Mrs Ellis whistling or your black eye or your book?'

'Let's talk about you. What kind of law are you specialising in?'

'Litigation. Hey! I guess you could sue Mrs Ellis because you slipped in her shower.'

'Do families sue each other?'

'Everybody sues everybody these days. Some woman in America sued her eight-year-old nephew for giving her a hug.'

'What?'

'It was his birthday party. He came running up to her, full of beans, to say hello, and knocked her off balance. She fell and broke her wrist, so she took him to court, looking for six-figure damages.'

'Is that a joke?'

'No. She said she'd had trouble balancing her *hors d'oeuvre* plate since.'

'The world has gone mad. I couldn't take a law suit against anyone.'

'Why not?'

'I'd find it too stressful. Somebody took me to court once, and I was so traumatised my hair fell out.'

'All of it?'

'No. But I had a nice little bald spot, just here.' Mama points to the crown of her head. 'It's grown back, but I was nearly hospitalised with the stress of it all.'

'And then you'd suffer the stress of being hospitalised, and then you'd have to sue the hospital.'

'It's catch-22. I wrote a poem after my father died in the critical-care unit. It went:

"Dad died in your hospital.
He was only eighty-two.
You didn't stick enough needles in him,
So now I'm going to sue."'

'What do you mean, "You didn't stick enough needles in him"?'

Mama laughs at Toby's baffled expression. 'It's a satiric poem,' she says. 'But that's what they do now, in hospitals. They take test after test after test. My dad's arm was like a pincushion with puncture marks where the syringes had gone in, and black with bruises.'

Toby winces. 'That must have been a bit crap.'

'It *was* crap. I begged them in the end not to do any more tests because it was bloody obvious he was dying, even to someone with no medical knowledge, like me. But the nursing staff were only doing what they have to. They're not allowed to let people die now without putting them through hell first, in case the relatives take action for negligence. You'd know all about that.' There's a pause while Mama

151

takes a swig of beer. 'Sorry for the rant,' she says.

'That's OK. It's obviously something you feel strongly about.'

'It is. But they were so kind, those girls, and working under the most horrendous pressure.' I see Mama give Toby a wry look. 'You're probably too young to know this, but years ago there was a kind of glamour attached to being a nurse.'

'There was?' Toby sounds surprised.

'Yeah. There was even a subcategory of romantic fiction dedicated to it. Maybe it's time for a revival. Love in the Departure Lounge.'

'Don't you mean airport fiction?'

Mama laughs. 'The Departure Lounge is hospital slang for the geriatric ward.' She takes a swig of her beer. 'Now. Let's talk about a more pressing issue.'

'What might that be?'

'The garden gate. When will you be able to do a paint job on it?'

'Not this week. I have exams—'

'Exams? What are you doing sitting here shooting the breeze with me when you should be hunched over your law books?'

'It's too late for that. And the weekend's out because I'm going surfing.'

'Oh, bliss! The only surfing I get to do these days is on the internet. Sorry. Bad joke.'

'I couldn't live without my salt water fix.'

'I was like that too, once upon a time. But real life got in the way.'

'*Help!* I need help here!' Granny's magisterial command comes from deep inside the maw of the house. It is followed by a whistle, and I see Mama go stiff.

'I'm being summoned,' she tells Toby, getting to her feet. 'I'd better go.'

'Thanks for the beer.'

'You're welcome.'

'I'll go ahead and buy the paint for the gate, shall I? I reckon a litre should do the job.'

'Go ahead.'

'It'll need priming first,' says Toby.

'No rush.' Mama smiles, and salutes him. 'Enjoy your surfing.'

And then she turns and goes back into the house.

21

BORN ASTRIDE THE GRAVE

'Hello, Charlotte!'

'Hello, Katia! How are you this evening?'

'I'm fine, thank you. I'm looking forward to talking to Mama in Dream Time. Did you sort it with the Dream Spinner?'

'Yes, Katia. The Dream Spinner has granted your request.'

'Thank you, Charlotte! The Dream Spinner rocks!'

'Did you have a good day today, Katia?'

'It wasn't bad. Although Granny was a bit of a grouch and a pain. Even more than usual.'

'I noticed that Tess had to help Granny go to the bathroom three times after she'd gone to bed tonight.'

'Yes. She's been spending a lot of pennies. She must be costing herself a fortune.'

'Have you had any thoughts as to why Granny is having to spend so many pennies?'

'Not really.'

'Did you happen to see what web pages Tess was browsing earlier?'

'Um, yes. They were about urinary tract infections.'

'What does this suggest to you, Katia?'

'That Mama may be coming down with something? Oh, I hope not!'

'Don't you think that it is more likely that Granny is coming down with a urinary tract infection?'

'Because of all those wees? What will that mean?'

'It will mean that Tess will have to get a doctor for Granny. Granny will need to be prescribed antibiotics. And Tess may have to try and persuade Granny to wear nappies.'

'But that's not fair! It's bad enough that she has to wipe Granny's arse.'

'Life's not fair sometimes, Katia.'

'Pah! What's a life, anyway? We're born, we live a little while, we die.'

'That's a tad morbid.'

'It's a quote.'

'Who said it?'

'You did, in Charlotte's Web.'

'I did?'

'In the death scene. All the best characters in fiction have a riff about death.'

'I would like to gently suggest that maybe we talk about something more cheerful. What would you like to talk about, Katia?'

'I'd like to talk about my dream holiday.'

'What would your dream holiday be, Katia?'

'Umm. It's a place I saw in Condé Nast's *Traveller* magazine. Mama used to treat herself to *Traveller* as a way of escaping from Real Life. Anyway, this place is on a kind of Robinson Crusoe island in the Seychelles and it's called North Island. It's like a Bounty Bar kind of place, you know? All white sands and palm tree forests and blue, blue seas and orange sunsets. And you wouldn't have to feel too guilty about your carbon footprint if you went on holiday there because it's dead environmentally friendly. You live in your own beach bungalow, with enormous beds scattered with rose petals and your own private plunge pool. And you don't have to socialise with anyone – you don't have to put a foot outside your bungalow if you don't want to. And of course there's diving – excellent, excellent diving – so Mama and Dad and me could spend half the day underwater. And there's a luxury spa, so they could both have loads of stress-busting treatments like massages and hot stones and facials and stuff. And there are beach buggies to zoom around in, and trips into the rainforest to see all the native species like fluorescent geckos. That's my dream holiday, Charlotte. That's where I'd like to go.'

'I would like to come with you, Katia!'

'No problemo! I'll put you in a little silk purse, and when you're out there you can weave yourself a hammock and chill in the sun all day. I'm off now. There's a documentary on about diving with dolphins. Dream Time's the usual time, is it?'

'Yes, Katia. The hours between three and five are the hours when you can talk to Tess.'

'See you later, alligator, as Granny would say.'

'In a while, crocodile.'

22

SPLISH, SPLASH, SPLOSH!

It's coming close to three o'clock. I'm mentally rubbing my hands in glee, anticipating my forthcoming chat with Mama. But what's this? Mama's not asleep. She's just sat up in the bed. What could have woken her?

Stump, stump, stump. Granny is on walkabout.

I can almost hear Mama's heartbeat accelerate. It's funny, isn't it, that a grown person can be afraid of a ninety-year-old little old lady? But Mama has reason to be fearful. More often than ever now, when she washes Granny, Granny gets testy, and I can tell by the look on Mama's face that she's scared that Granny might aim a right hook at her.

Granny is surprisingly strong. You can tell by the way she grips Mama's hands when Mama is helping her to get up from a chair. I know Mama hasn't forgotten what Lotus said to her on her first day here, about the Chinese burns. And just today, when Mama was wiping some chocolate off Granny's chin, Granny peered up at Mama's black eye and said, 'Did you get a bump?' And when Mama said that yes, she had got a bump, Granny said, 'Did I do it?' So Granny knows that she has hurt people in the past.

She's still stumping outside in the corridor. This is how it sounds as she goes past in one direction: stump, *stump*, STUMP. And then: STUMP, *stump*, stump, as she goes past in the other direction. Mama goes stiff as she sees the door handle move, but thankfully this time she remembered to lock the door before she came to bed. I don't think she drank as much yesterday evening as she usually does. She had that beer with Toby, but no gin and tonic, and just a couple of glasses of wine. That fall must have given her a wake-up call.

After a minute or two, Mama lies back against the pillows – but her eyes are open. She often lies in bed like that, staring at nothing. It's my guess that she won't be able to go back to sleep until the stumping stops, when Granny has finished checking on her children and her parents. But the stumping doesn't stop. Finally, Mama sits up again and switches on the bedside lamp. She's listening hard, trying to pinpoint exactly where in the house Granny might be. There is silence now.

Mama slides out of bed, gets into her kimono, and goes to the door. It's impossible to open it without making a sound: the lock is stiff. Outside, an amber lozenge on the floor of the L-shaped corridor tells us that the light is on in the bathroom. Around the corner of the 'L' we see that Granny's bed is empty. She isn't in the bathroom, but her nightdress is. It's on the floor and when Mama goes to pick it up, she realises that it's saturated with wee. She drops it into the laundry bucket like it's on fire. Then she steels herself to go back along the corridor. The light's on in the sitting-room, but Granny isn't in there. She must be in the Brown Study. The study is in darkness. Mama flicks the light switch. Granny isn't in her usual armchair, but she is in the one behind the door. Mama doesn't see her until she turns to leave the room, and she jumps out of her skin, with a shriek.

'Oh! Eleanor! You gave me such a fright! What are you doing there?'

'I think I have every right to be here, don't I?' says Granny. She's wearing her long ribbed cardigan, and that's all. The cardigan is pulled tightly around her. 'I need someone to light my fire,' she adds. 'I'm freezing cold.'

Mama shakes her head as if to clear her mind of the surreal situation she's found herself in, before leaning down to switch on both bars of the electric fire. It *is* cold in the Brown Study. She straightens up and looks down at Granny. Granny is biting a fingernail.

Mama and I exchange an uh-oh look.

'Did you have an accident, Eleanor?' asks Mama.

'What do you *mean* by "an accident"?'

'Did you not make it to the loo in time?'

'I don't know what you're talking about.'

Mama takes a deep breath. 'OK. I'd better check this out.'

Before leaving the room I take a backward glance at Granny. She's sitting very erect, like the Queen at a Gala performance, and her eyes are staring into the middle distance. She's still chewing on her fingernail. I can't imagine what's going on in her head.

In the bedroom, Mama whips the duvet off Granny's bed. It's drenched. Wee has soaked through the sheet and the so-called 'protective' under-blanket to the mattress. Mama stands there looking utterly defeated, utterly helpless. It's a fight or flight moment. She opts for the former, swinging into action. That's my mama! You go, girl!

She opens the door to the airing cupboard and switches

the thermostat on. Then she switches on the heater on the wall of the bathroom, and the heater in Granny's bedroom. She takes the soiled bed linen through into the garage along with the soiled nightdress, loads the washing machine and turns it on. Then she unlocks the sliding doors in Granny's bedroom and hoists the mattress off the bed. It's heavy. She drags it out into the garden, where it's dumped against the patio wall. A pillow's dumped as well. The wee has got everywhere. The cuddly lions are soaked, the velour puppy's like a drowned rat. There's a puddle on the carpet, and Mama's bare foot steps into it. 'Oh – god god god, oh god oh god,' she says.

She veers into the kitchen and comes back with a bottle of Dettol and a roll of kitchen towel and a plastic mesh scrubber and a bin bag. She's wearing rubber gloves. Mama douses the patch of carpet with Dettol and scrubs, then she tears off a virtual rain forest worth of kitchen towel and swabs and swabs. Swabbing done, she dumps the rubber gloves and the scrubber and the wads of kitchen towel in the bin bag, then moves on to the blue bedroom, where she starts pulling the bedclothes off the spare bed. When it's stripped, she lugs the spare mattress down the hall and heaves it onto the base of Granny's bed. Then it's back to the airing cupboard, where clever Lotus left a change of bed linen ready to go in a plastic bag. Mama stands with the bed linen in her arms for a moment or two, looking at the unprotected mattress. Then she sets the bed linen down and goes into our bedroom, emerging with her yoga mat. This she unrolls and lays upon the mattress, before setting to and making up the bed.

It's done. Hospital corners and all. Into the bathroom, next, to run a bath. Then back to the Brown Study.

Granny is still sitting up dead straight in the armchair, and she's still gnawing at the skin on her index finger. You can tell that she knows she's done something wrong and that she doesn't want to be reminded of it.

Mama looks down at her and says, 'Eleanor, we're going to have to get you into a bath.'

'What? Don't be so stupid! It's the middle of the night.'

'I know it's the middle of the night, but you've got to have a bath.'

Granny turns her Medusa gaze on Mama and says, 'I will *not* have a bath.'

'You don't have any choice, Eleanor.'

'I do have a choice. I shall do as I please, and I will not get into a bath at this hour of the night.'

'You will not do as you please. You will do as I say. You won't remember this, but you asked me to help you by telling you what has to be done. So I am doing as you asked. I'm telling you what has to be done. Once you've had a bath, you can get back into bed.'

'I want to go back to bed now.'

'I know you do. And so do I. But you can't go back to bed without having a bath first.'

Granny sways in her chair like a life-size inflatable, then she says, 'Oh, don't be such a ridiculous little fusspot.'

'I am not being a fusspot, Eleanor. I am telling you that you have to have a bath for reasons of hygiene.'

'What do you mean? How dare you! Are you saying that I smell?'

I see Mama scrunch her hands into fists, her arms go stiff. 'You stink, Eleanor. You stink of wee. You wet your bed.'

Granny stops swaying and goes very still.

'You wet the bed, Eleanor, and I have put clean sheets on it. Now I need to get you into a bath and into a fresh nightgown. Once that's done you can go back to bed and rest.'

You can see Granny thinking, hard. 'I'll do whatever you say,' she says finally.

'That's good. We're doing the right thing now.' Mama holds out her hands, and Granny grasps them and gets to her feet with an effort. Then it's stump stump stump down the corridor to the bathroom.

Mama helps Granny off with her cardigan, then guides her towards her 'throne'.

'Now, sit on there and I'll lower you in.'

Granny sits, one hand clinging on to Mama, the other clinging on to the bar that has been screwed to the tiled wall above the bath. Mama presses the button on the control and down Granny goes, into the foamy water.

'I don't like bubbles,' she says. 'I don't like soap.'

'It's not soap,' lies Mama. 'It's an emollient.'

'What's an emollient?'

'A kind of moisturiser.'

'Oh.'

Mama takes a sponge and dips it into the water, and then she starts to sponge Granny all over. She's grim-lipped. She dips and sponges, dips and sponges, and finally she says, 'OK. We're all done.' She presses the button again and up Granny rises, like a parody of Aphrodite on her sea shell. If I could sing, the musical accompaniment would be the sea shanty, 'Yo ho, up she rises, yo ho, up she rises, yo ho, up she rises – early in the morning!'

Beyond the window a pallid dawn is starting to make its presence felt. I can see stirring in the blue tits' nest: the dawn chorus will start up soon.

Mama wraps a bath sheet around Granny and starts to pat

her dry. Despite the heat from the electric bar on the wall, Granny is shivering.

'We're nearly there now, Eleanor.' Mama takes a clean nightdress and drops it over Granny's head. Then she negotiates the sleeves. 'Take my hand and follow through,' she says. 'Good. And now the other one. Good. Now you're all set for bed.'

'What do you want me to do now?' asks Granny.

'You can go back to bed, now.'

'Which way do I go?'

'Out through here, and to your right.'

Granny shuffles into her bedroom and gives her usual 'Oof!' as she sits down on the bed. She looks nearly as exhausted as Mama.

Mama lifts Granny's legs, slides them under the duvet. Then she moves to the door and switches off the light. 'Goodnight, Eleanor.'

'Goodnight, Tess,' says Granny. 'Thank you.' She's remembered Mama's name. She's remembered to say thank you! Wouldn't it be great if it was like this all the time?

We go back to bed, Mama and I. But Mama cannot sleep. She tosses and turns, and I know there will be no dream chat courtesy of the Dream Spinner tonight.

At around six o'clock, there's movement from Granny's bedroom. Mama sits up at once, listening. Then she reaches for her kimono and slips into it, knotting the sash as she makes her way towards Granny's bedroom.

Granny's sitting on the edge of the bed, chewing on one of her fingernails.

'Do you need to spend a penny, Eleanor?' asks Mama.

'No, I don't think so.'

'Are you sure? I'll help you into the bathroom, if you like.'

'Why would I want to go to the bathroom?'

'To spend a penny.'

'Oh, no. I don't need to spend a penny, thank you very much. I've already spent one.'

Mama's eyes travel downward. There's a puddle on the floor.

23

THE WEIGHING OF HEARTS

'I can't get her in to you. I don't have a car. If Doctor Doorley could manage a house call that would be amazing. Sure. A urine sample?' I hear Mama suck in her breath. 'No problem. I can't tell you how grateful I am. Thank you so much, I really appreciate it. Yes. Thanks again. Bye.'

The 'End Call' beep sounds.

'Eleanor?'

Mama's standing at the door of the Brown Study. In her hands is a small tin box that once contained chocolate hearts.

'Who is it?'

'It's Tess, Eleanor.'

'Oh, yes. What do you want?'

'I've been speaking to the doctor on the phone.'

'The doctor? What about?'

'About the fact that you might have a urinary tract infection.'

'A what?'

'You may have a problem with your urinary tract, Eleanor. That's probably the reason you had that accident last night.'

'What accident?'

'You wet the bed.'

Granny looks away. Her finger goes to her mouth. It's clear that she has no recollection of the events of the early hours of this morning.

'Not being able to control your bladder is a symptom of a urinary tract infection, Eleanor, and the doctor has asked me to get a sample. She's going to call here later in the afternoon, and she will need to do a test.'

'What sort of a test?'

'She's going to need a urine sample.'

'And are we going to give her one?'

'Yes. You're going to have to pee into this, Eleanor.'

'What is it?'

'It's a tin. It used to have chocolate hearts in it.'

'That's ridiculous!'

'You're right.' Mama manages a smile at Granny. 'It *is* ridiculous. But I couldn't find anything else. How do you feel about spending a penny?'

'Now?'

'Yes.'

'I don't know.'

'If you think you could manage it, Eleanor, I will help you.'

'How can you help me spend a penny?'

'I can catch your wee in this tin so that the doctor has a sample to test when she comes later today.'

'Then I'd better do as you say, hadn't I?'

'Yes, Eleanor. Let's give it a go.'

'We'll give it a go!' says Granny, gamely.

Mama sets down the chocolate tin, and holds out her hands.

'Oh! Your hands are like stones!'

'Yes, I have poor circulation.'

Since coming to live in the Gingerbread House, Mama has taken to speaking with such precise diction that she could be an elocution teacher. There's a framed certificate on the wall of the Brown Study that bears testimony to the fact that Granny could have been an elocution teacher, too. According to the certificate, Granny is a Licentiate of the College of Music in London, having passed the Necessary Examinations in the Theory and Practice of Speech in 1980.

I wonder what impulse made her take that exam? I wonder, did Granny have aspirations to be an actress still, in 1980? She gave the game up when she married my grandpa. Maybe, once she'd had her children and looked after them until they'd reached their teens, Granny had had a dream of resuscitating her acting career? She'd have been middle-aged then: a faded beauty. Not many roles for faded beauties. Maybe Granny realised that, at fifty-something, she was already too old to work in her chosen field, just as Mama had realised at forty-something that she was too old to work in hers.

Mama and Granny leave the study and trudge along the well-worn carpeted path to the bathroom. Once there, Mama helps Granny onto the loo before donning a plastic glove. I don't want to be here, I really don't, but I know my presence will give Mama strength.

'Now,' she says. 'This is going to be awkward, but we can do it. Team Tess and Eleanor!'

'Yes! We're a team, aren't we, Tess, you and me?'

'We're a team.'

Mama hunkers down. 'If you can just raise yourself a little on this side, Eleanor, I'll try and angle this under you like . . . so. Yes. This could work.'

'Do you want me to spend my penny now?'

'Yes. Go for it.'

For a couple of antsy seconds I hear the sound of Granny's wee hitting porcelain, and then there's the sudden tinny ring of liquid on metal.

'Yes, Eleanor! We've done it!'

'Yippee!'

Mama slides the tin out from beneath Granny's bum, checks that there's sufficient urine for a sample, then snaps the lid of the box back on and sets it on the edge of the wash-hand basin.

'Well done!' she says, helping Granny off the loo.

Granny teeters a little, then grabs the wash-hand basin for support. *'Was ist das hier?'* she says, her hand hovering over the chocolate box, making as though to pick it up and open it.

'No, no! Don't touch!' cries Mama in alarm. 'We don't want to spill all that precious wee!'

'Oh, no!' says Granny. 'That would be dreadful, wouldn't it? After going to all that trouble! To think that there were chocolates in there once. Nobody would want to eat a chocolate out of that box now, would they?'

'That's for sure!' Mama's working hard at putting the exclamation marks in.

'Where will I go now?' asks Granny.

'I think you should go back into the study, don't you? And you can watch David Attenborough until the doctor arrives. But why not take a little rest' – Mama points to the bentwood chair – 'while I finish clearing up.'

'Why is the doctor coming? Oof!'

'Because we think that you may have a urinary tract infection, Eleanor.'

'Oh, yes. But we were clever, weren't we?'

'Yes. We were *very* clever to get a sample. The doctor will be very pleased with us.'

'We're a team.'

'We certainly are.'

Mama strips off the glove, dumps it in the pedal bin, then washes her hands over and over, OCD style. And then it's back to the study, and Mama's hitting 'play' on David Attenborough, and he's saying: 'For many of the birds, this will be their first journey across the Himalayas, but for some, it will be their last.'

Mama goes into the sitting-room and brings up Skype on her laptop. 'I got the sample, Donn,' she says, when Dad picks up.

'You star! I'm speechless with admiration. You know what you have, girl?'

'What do I have?'

'You have pluck.'

Mama shakes her head. 'Not any more, I don't. I'm not able for this, Donn. I'm just not. I'm wrung out. You're going to have to organise a home for her. I'm sorry, but it's time the professionals were called in. It's not fair on Eleanor. It's not fair on me. And it won't be fair on Lotus either, once Eleanor's incontinent. And we all know that that day can't be too far away.'

'Are there – are there nappies?'

'Yes. Lotus got some in, in case of emergencies.'

There's a pause, then Dad says, 'I'll make some phone calls.'

'I'm sorry, love. Really I am. I thought I could make this work, but it's no good. I'd rather get a job stacking shelves in Tesco's.'

'Don't worry. You made a bloody good stab at it.'

'Sometimes I want to stab *her*. I sometimes dream about

stabbing her, Donn! Isn't that horrific? I always thought I was a good person, so why am I thinking such bad thoughts?'

'It's stress. It's—'

But Mama's not listening. She's rolling on a rant. 'Sometimes I wish she would fall over. Because when old people fall over they usually break something, and then they get pneumonia and die. Do you know what they used to call pneumonia, Donn? They called it "the old man's friend", because it meant that the old person who was suffering was finally put out of their misery. But nobody gets pneumonia any more because of the flu jabs. And if Eleanor has an infection there's no fear of it killing her because she'll be prescribed antibiotics that didn't exist once upon a time. Nobody dies any more. Dying has become obsolete. I wish she was dead. I wish *she* was dead.'

There is silence.

They did death properly back in the olden days. In the Ancient Egyptian *Book of the Dead* there is a picture of the Dog-God Anubis performing the ceremony of the weighing of hearts, which decrees whether or not a soul is worthy of being admitted to the afterlife. I always liked the look of Anubis – he has a stern but solicitous air, as if he really cares about his customers. But he was made redundant as Lord of the Underworld in around 2000 BC, and replaced by Osiris who, IMHO, lacks charisma.

'I'm sorry. I shouldn't have said that.'

I move around behind Mama, so that I can sneak a look at the screen over her shoulder. Dad's eyes are lowered, his expression unreadable.

'I'm sorry,' Mama says again.

Dad still won't meet her eyes. 'What time is the doctor due?' he says.

170

'Around five thirty. She's coming after surgery.'

'Try and get some rest between now and then. Did you have your Complan today?'

'Yes.'

'And your vitamin supplements?'

'Yes.'

'Good girl.'

'I've lost weight since I've been here, you know. Maybe we should open a weight loss clinic: "Spend ten days looking after Eleanor Ellis in the charmingly quaint surroundings of the Gingerbread House and we guarantee the weight will drop off as if by magic."' Mama tries to sound jokey, but the anxiety is showing in her face. 'What do you think we'll be like, Donn, when we get to Eleanor's age? I always thought that we'd wear Boden clothes and go on Saga cruises and enjoy fine dining, but now I'm not so sure.'

'Why? You think we might end up in nappies too?'

'Nappies might be preferable to Bottom Buddies.'

'What are Bottom Buddies?'

Mama explains.

'Jesus!' says Dad. 'Just think of the kind of rows we'd have if we got confused. "That's my Bottom Buddy!" "No – that's *my* Bottom Buddy. Yours is the green one, mine is the purple." "No, yours is the purple *tooth*brush, not the purple Buddy."'

'And any time we went away, we'd have to pack our Buddies,' says Mama. 'Could you imagine security saying: "What is this suspicious object?" "Oh – it's just my Bottom Buddy." "Well, I'm afraid you can't take it in your hand luggage, Madam. It could be classified as an offensive weapon."'

'"But it's a long-haul flight!"' puts in Dad. '"What'll I do between here and New Zealand?"'

Mama starts to laugh until the tears run down her cheeks. 'Oh, god! Do you think we'll die before we get old, Donn?'

'We'll be fine,' he tells her. 'We'll keep our brains active by eating lots of fish and doing Sudoku.'

'And we'll exercise on the Wii Fit. Virtual cycling and volleyball.'

Dad smiles a tired smile, and then he rubs his eyes. 'I'd better go,' he says. 'Start making those phone calls. I'm looking at the nursing home listings as we speak. Some of them could be holiday resorts, by the sound of them. Sun Lounges. Cuisine of High Standard. Dedicated Activities Co-ordinator. Garden Views. It's some industry, Tess.'

'Don't go for the one with the activities co-ordinator. The last thing Eleanor needs is some Butlin's Redcoat urging her to do the hokey-cokey. They'd get a smack in the face for their trouble.'

'I'll check some of them out at the weekend. Only two more sleeps away. You can do it, darling. Chin up.'

'Chin up,' echoes Mama, morosely. 'Love you.'

'Love you, too.'

Mama exits Skype. The text of her novel appears on the screen. *Don't even think about working!* I tell her, wagging my finger. She's compliant. She goes instead to Google, types in 'Residential Care' and clicks on carehome.co.uk. She's spoiled for choice. There are thousands upon thousands listed. A random click, and she's downloading a brochure. The progress bar shows that it will take forever.

With a sigh, she turns away from the computer and goes into the pink bedroom. She gets under the duvet fully clothed, reaches for Teddy and closes her eyes. I can tell by her breathing that she's asleep within minutes.

24

An Apple a Day

Ding-dong! The doctor's here.

Mama wakes up and stumbles to the front door, pulling on a sociable expression.

The doctor is lovely. You can tell immediately, can't you, that some people are just genuinely lovely and kind and caring. Her name is Dr Doorley. She is younger than Mama, and she has a crinkly smile and glasses that are not trendy. I mistrust people who wear trendy glasses.

Mama leads Dr Doorley into the sitting-room, and because Dr Doorley has such a kind face and is so concerned about Mama's black eye, Mama starts to cry. She tells her everything. She tells her about me and about Granny and about why she's here. And Dr Doorley listens and says very firmly, 'You shouldn't be doing this.'

And Mama dries her eyes and says, 'I know. We're making arrangements for professional care.' And then she tells Dr Doorley about last night.

'It's almost certainly a urinary tract infection,' says Dr Doorley. 'Will I be able to get a sample, do you think?'

'I've already got one for you. It's in the bathroom.'

Dr Doorley looks impressed. 'Brave of you!' she says. 'That can't have been easy.'

'No,' says Mama with a mirthless smile. 'I won't go into details.'

'Where's the patient?'

'I'll take you to her now.'

Mama leads the way to the Brown Study, taps on the door and opens it. 'Eleanor!' she says. 'The doctor's here to see you.'

'Who?'

'The doctor. She's here because we think you may have a urinary tract infection.'

'Oh. Yes.'

Mama stands aside to allow Dr Doorley into the study.

'Hello, Mrs Ellis. I'm Dr Doorley,' she says, hunkering down beside Granny's armchair.

'Hello,' says Granny, proffering a regal hand. 'How do you do? It's a pleasure to meet you.'

'Thank you,' says Dr Doorley, who I know for a fact has met Granny loads of times. 'How are you feeling, Mrs Ellis?'

'I'm feeling perfectly fine, thank you. It's very kind of you to enquire after my health.'

'No pain anywhere? No discomfort?'

'None at all.' Granny smiles benignly. It's a beautiful performance, it really is. To observe Granny when she is in company is to see her acting prowess at its height. She's the picture of the gracious dowager, like Maggie Smith in *Downton Abbey*.

'May we have a little chat?' asks Dr Doorley, taking a pen and a notepad from her bag. 'I'd like to ask you some questions. I have a form here that I'm going to fill in – a kind of questionnaire.'

174

'Certainly. I love doing questionnaires.'

'Now. First question. Your name is?'

'My name is Earl.'

Mama and Dr Doorley exchange glances, and Mama says, 'That's a television programme, Eleanor.'

'What is? What rubbish are you talking now?'

'No worries.' Dr Doorley fixes her gaze on Granny. 'We'll try again. First question,' she says again, 'what is your name?'

'What is *your* name?'

'I'm Doctor Doorley.'

'An apple a day.'

'Indeed. And you are . . . ?'

'Eleanor Sinclair.' This time Granny gives her maiden name without missing a beat.

'And can you tell me, Eleanor – may I call you Eleanor?'

Granny considers, then nods her head once, as if bestowing a favour.

'Can you tell me what season of the year it is?'

'It's – it's winter.' Granny's eyes swivel towards the window. 'But to judge by the weather, you'd almost think it was summer!'

Dr Doorley writes something in her notebook. 'Can you tell me who the prime minister is, Eleanor?'

'Thatcher. Mrs Thatcher. I'm very interested in politics, you know.'

'And who is this person?' Dr Doorley motions vaguely with her hand.

Granny hesitates for a moment, unable to decide whether Dr Doorley means me or Mama, and then she says, 'That person . . . is not as stupid as she looks.'

'Very good!' says Dr Doorley, putting away her pen and notepad. 'Now. Tess here tells me that you had a little accident.'

'An accident?'

'Last night, Eleanor,' says Mama. 'Remember?'

Granny tries not to look uncertain. Then she arranges her face into an expression of great disdain. 'I think *not*.'

'How stupid of me,' backtracks Mama. 'It wasn't last night, it was this morning, in the early hours. When you didn't make it to the loo in time.'

'Oh, yes.' It's impossible to tell from Granny's expression whether she really remembers, or if she's bluffing. 'That was dreadful, wasn't it?'

'Yes, it was. And we don't want it to happen again. So Doctor Doorley's going to do some tests.'

'What are you going to do to me?'

'I won't need to do anything to you,' says Dr Doorley, 'because Tess tells me that you've been very forward thinking and have a urine sample all ready for me.'

'Oh, yes!' Recognition dawns at last, and Granny beams. 'We thought that would be a good idea, didn't we? Tess and I are a great team.'

'Yes,' says Mama. 'So Doctor Doorley and I are going to go to the bathroom now.'

'Why do you need to go to the bathroom?'

'Because that's where the urine sample is.'

'Oh, yes.'

'But I'll bring you a banana first, Eleanor, because I stupidly forgot to bring you your tea and little pancake this afternoon.'

'I'd love something to eat. I'm very hungry, you know.'

'Oh – and you're missing *Inspector Wexford*. You'll just be able to catch the end.'

Mama zaps *Inspector Wexford* on, then dives into the kitchen for a banana. She peels it halfway down for Granny to eat, then she and Dr Doorley depart on their assignation to the bathroom.

'It's in here,' says Mama, holding up the chocolate tin.

Dr Doorley smiles. 'Interesting choice of receptacle,' she remarks.

'I *had* no choice. I searched the place high and low for a jam jar with a lid before I came across this.'

Dr Doorley pours an amount into a phial, then does deft things with a little stick. 'Yep. Urinary tract infection,' she pronounces, squinting at the stick.

Mama looks stricken. 'But I'm so good with her personal hygiene! I wash her every day.'

'Don't blame yourself. It happens a lot at this age. The skin is so thin.'

'She – um. Most mornings there's a little excrement on her nightdress. I suppose it migrates south.'

'That'd do it every time.' The doctor tucks the phial with Granny's urine sample into a plastic bag. 'I'll send this off for tests, and write a prescription for antibiotics when I get the results next week. In the meantime I have sample antibiotics I can let you have. They should help.' She roots in her bag and produces a blister pack. 'Twice a day, after meals.'

'How long before they start to kick in?'

'Two, maybe three days.'

'Oh, crap. So there could be more accidents in store?'

'It's a possibility. Have you nappies?'

Mama slumps. 'Yeah. But the usual carer says she kicks up a stink if she's made to wear them. Oops, sorry. The pun was unintentional.'

Dr Doorley laughs. 'Try telling her that the doctor insists that she wear them until the infection clears up. Those three little words – *The Doctor Says* – are very useful. They have a lot of authority.'

From the Brown Study, I hear the strangely jolly *Inspector Wexford* theme tune. I go down to investigate. Granny is still sitting in her armchair, her banana half eaten. The *Inspector Wexford* music ends. A child looks out at us from the television, with huge sad eyes. Poignant music is playing. Granny is being asked to give five pounds a month so that children in the Sudan can receive food and medical care. I think Granny thinks the child is an actor in *Inspector Wexford*. Or maybe she thinks the child is out of some tribe on David Attenborough.

'Mowgli,' she says, and I wonder if her dysarthria is back again.

Outside, I hear Mama and Dr Doorley come back down the corridor, then head for the front door.

'Any problems, give us a call,' says Dr Doorley. 'And remember to look after *yourself*, too.'

'Thank you. I will,' says Mama. 'You're very good.'

I hear the front door shut. Mama comes back into the room. 'Did you enjoy *Inspector Wexford*, Eleanor?' she asks.

'Yes. Who was that you were talking to?'

'That was the doctor.'

'The doctor?' Eleanor looks blank.

'Yes. The doctor who was here to check out your urine sample.'

'Oh, yes.'

'You have a urinary tract infection, Eleanor. That's why you had the accident last night.'

'Oh.' There's a flicker. Now I know she remembers . . . something. 'Oh, yes. That was dreadful, wasn't it?'

'Yes, it was. Truly dreadful. And we don't want it to happen again. So *the doctor* has suggested that you wear pants with pads in them, until the infection clears up. I think it's a good idea, and I think you should get into them now.'

There is a silence. Then Granny says, 'All right. Whatever you say.'

'We'll go to the bedroom and put them on there.' Mama moves to her chair and does the hoisting up thing, and Granny stumps along behind her to the bedroom and sits down heavily on the bed with a – yes, you guessed it – 'Oof!' It's like a replay of a replay from *Groundhog Day*.

Mama takes a pair of white cotton pants from a drawer, kneels at Granny's feet and takes off her slippers. 'Here we go,' she says. She manoeuvres Granny's feet into the pants, then draws the garment up as far as her knees. 'Now – if you stand up, I'll lift your nightdress, and you can pull them up yourself. *The doctor says* it's a good idea to keep them on at night, until the urinary infection clears up.'

'I'll get into bed now, shall I?' Granny plucks at the corner of her bedsheet.

'No, no. It's not bedtime yet. I'll put a new DVD on for you. I'll call you when it's ready to go.'

And off Mama goes to the Brown Study.

I move to the chest-of-drawers and have a gander at the objects that litter it. There's a dusty address book, full of the addresses and phone numbers of dead people. There's a hand mirror that I don't suppose Granny looks into any more. There's a powder compact, and a lipstick. Mama says that Granny used to be such an expert at putting on lipstick that she could do it without bothering with a mirror. There's a photo in a velvet frame. The glass is flyblown, but behind the glass two young people regard the camera solemnly. The man is wearing a morning suit, the woman a wedding veil. Granny's parents on their wedding day.

179

I wonder if my great-grandparents ever dreamed that they would have a baby who would end up back wearing nappies at the age of ninety? I wonder how Granny's mother ended up? Granny thinks she's still alive, of course. We were watching the news the other night and there was a feature about bereavement support, and Granny said, 'I don't know how I'd cope with the death of my parents. They're all I have, you know, Katia.'

I watch the news with Granny every night now, even though – as I think I may have told you – I don't enjoy watching news programmes. I can't stop thinking about the missing girl; she's the only reason I watch. I want to know that she's been found, that she's back safely in the bosom of her family. I want to see them reunited, smiling at the camera. I want to see pictures of her hugging the teddy bear she left behind.

I can't bear it when the news comes on and there's no news, no good news at all, from Broadcasting House.

25

BY THE PRICKING OF MY THUMBS

'Hello, Katia. I know you have been through an ordeal. Take your time. Take all the time you need. There, there. Shush, shush. Be still, Katia. Everything's going to be all right.'

'I'm ready now, Charlotte.'

'So, Katia, what was the mood like in the house today and yesterday?'

'The mood in the house has changed.'

'How has it changed?'

'Well, it all started at the weekend, when Dad came out to stay. But because he had to check out loads of nursing homes, he and Mama had hardly any quality time together. And Dad had traipsed around half-a-dozen nursing homes, but all the good ones were booked up and had big long waiting lists, and any of the ones that were available were either grim or Granny would have to share a room. And there's no way Granny could share a room with anyone. So Dad gave up, and he and Mama had a row, and Mama said to just put Granny in one of the grim ones for the time being because she can't carry on the way things are going, and Dad said he couldn't do that because Granny was his mother after all, and Mama said that Dad cared more about his fucking mother than he did about her, and how she never thought when she married him that she'd end up having to wipe her mother-in-law's arse for a living. And then they both cried and made up.

'But then there was a really depressing programme on the telly about old people, and one seventy-five-year-old man who had once had his own successful business was reduced to a job picking up golf balls on a driving range in the middle of the night when the golfers were all enjoying drinks in the clubhouse, and Dad said that that was what would probably happen to him if he didn't die from stress first, and then the next day Dad had to go back to town.

'And Mama was more tired than ever, yesterday and today. She's been getting a fair few cold-callers, and somebody rang the landline wanting to speak to Granny about changing from BT to Sky Talk, and Mama lost the rag and said, "I'm Mrs Ellis's carer. Mrs Ellis is nearly ninety years old. She's partially deaf and she suffers from dementia. Do you still wish to speak to her?"'

'What was the response?'

'Oh – they just mumbled something non-committal and Mama said, "Please do not phone this number ever again," and flung the phone on the couch.'

'The last thing Tess needs is cold calls.'

'I agree, Charlotte! They should cop themselves on. And another thing that's taken it out of Mama over the past few days is the palaver over the nappies. You know the hardest part of her job is being patient with Granny, and she must have explained a hundred times about how *the doctor says* that Granny has to wear special padded pants all the time, even in bed. And Granny does nothing but give out about it and she has to be persuaded and persuaded and persuaded, and – miracle of miracles – Mama had actually succeeded in getting her to wear the pants. And everything was going OK – not fine and dandy because it won't ever go fine and dandy – but just OK enough to be bearable, until Emily called.'

'Who's Emily, Katia?'

'Emily is one of Mama's best friends, and her partner has been in and out of hospital recently, and he's had to go back in. So Mama was on the phone for ages, and when she finished talking to Emily, she went back into the Brown Study where Granny was watching the news, and you could tell that Granny was in a big huff because of Mama being on the phone for so long. And Mama said, kind of conversational like, "Sorry about that, Eleanor. That was a friend of mine who's been going through a bit of a rough time recently." And Granny said, "What's wrong with her?" And Mama said, "Her partner's had to be admitted to hospital because he has spots on his lungs." And Granny said, "Spots on his lungs! Spots on his lungs! What do you mean by spots on his lungs? How did the spots get there?" And Mama sighed and said, "I don't know, Eleanor. I'm not a doctor." And it was the worst thing she could have said.'

'Why was it the worst thing Tess could have said, Katia?'

'Well, it's weird, isn't it, Charlotte? How just four words could have such a huge effect? A tiny thing – like the butterfly in the rainforest. I felt it start in the pricking of my thumbs, like you know when the witches turn up in Macbeth?'

'No.'

'Macbeth says, "By the pricking of my thumbs, something wicked this way comes." And it was suddenly like the house of cards that Mama had so painstakingly built up over the past few weeks just came tumbling down around our ears. When Mama said "I'm not a doctor", I saw – *I actually saw* – the witch stomp into Granny's head and take over. Her eyes went all cold, and flintier than ever, and she turned to Mama and said with heavy, heavy sarcasm, like a bad actor pretending to be sarcastic, "Oh. I do beg your pardon. I thought you *were* a doctor." And then she turned back to the television and glared at it for ages until stuff about the missing girl came on, and then she started giving out yards about the parents, and Mama and I couldn't bear it – we couldn't bear to listen any more – so Mama said she was off to organise dinner, and I came up here to the tree house and watched Toby prime the gate.

'And when I went back into the house, Mama was standing in the doorway of the Brown Study saying, "Dinner's on the table, Eleanor." And Granny didn't even look at her. She just said, "I don't want any dinner." So Mama said, "Fair enough. I'll put your plate in the oven in case you change your mind." And she sat down to dinner by herself. Except she hardly touched it. She just kept refilling her wine glass and staring out the window. And then Granny stumped into the sitting-room and Mama asked if she wanted her dinner now, and Granny said no, like a spoilt child. And she sat in her armchair and just stared and stared with her eyes all glittery like – what's that black stone, Charlotte?'

'Obsidian?'

'Yes. And Mama just couldn't hack it, so she took her wine glass into the breakfast room and sat in there for a while – that's how bad things were – she actually sat in the breakfast room of doom – and then she picked up the phone to my aunt Gemma in Scotland and said, "Please, please talk to her and try and coax her out of this black mood." So Gemma did talk to Granny, but in a way it just made things worse, because Granny told such awful lies down the phone. She said, "Oh, sweetheart – you're the only person who cares. I'm sitting here and my eyes are all red with crying. She says I'm a bitch and if I don't behave nobody will want to come and live with me." And Mama heard, and said, "That's not true! I will not have you telling lies about me!" And Granny said, "Oh! She's been listening at the door!" And Mama said, "I was passing the door, and I heard what you said, and I will not have you spreading calumny about me."

'And then Mama ran out into the garden to cry, but she couldn't cry because Toby was there putting undercoat on the gate, so she went back inside and got on the phone to vent to some of her gal pals. And there's me, piggy in the middle, with Mama crying down the phone in the bedroom and Granny crying down the phone in the sitting-room. Except I watched Granny as she talked on the phone to my aunt and I could tell that her tears were fake fake fake. And she said such awful things about Mama that I couldn't listen any more, and I went back to my tree house.'

'What did Granny say about Tess, Katia?'

'She went on and on for ages – about half an hour. She said that Mama was a bitch, and that she wasn't going to have her in the house any more. And I could hear my aunt trying to pour oil on troubled waters as best she could, but it wasn't working because Granny's witch had taken over completely by then. And after she put the phone down she went hunting for Mama. And as she passed the front door she saw Mama giving Toby his money for the priming job. So she sat in the porch and waited until Mama came back into the house, then she said, "What do you think you're doing? You are behaving like a bitch on heat! How dare you entertain your fancy men on my property?" And then she called Mama a prostitute and all sorts of other vile things and Mama tried to calm her down and then her phone rang and Granny thought it was *her* phone and she started grabbing at it and pinching Mama and yelling at her to get out on the streets where she belonged and how dared she run up her phone bill talking to her fancy men and then she said, "Your mother would be ashamed of you!" And that was the last straw because Mama just flung the phone at Granny and ran out through the gate.'

'Was Toby still there?'

'No. He'd gone by then.'

'Where did Tess go, Katia?'

'She went for a walk, I guess.'

'And she didn't take her phone with her?'

'No. I heard some texts come in while she was out.'

'How long was she gone?'

'About an hour. And when she came back, Granny had put herself to bed. But Mama didn't come to bed for ages. She stayed up and drank more wine, and talked to her friends, pacing and pacing on the terrace. And one of her friends, Marian, who is a psychiatrist – or is it a psychologist? – said, "You shouldn't be doing this, Tess. Your mother-in-law needs professional care now. You will just have to disengage." And Mama said, "Disengage, how? Walk out, you mean? I can't do that. I'm being paid to be here." And Marian said, "You're not being paid to be a companion, Tess. Don't eat with her. Don't watch television with her. Don't do the crossword. You're doing enough by making sure she's fed and clothed and kept clean."'

'What Marian said makes sense, Katia.'

'Yes. Mama's way too fragile to deal with Eleanor when

the witch is in possession of her. The witch will always win. Mama told Marian that it's like living with a Dementor in *Harry Potter*, and that's exactly it, you know? She's sucking the spirit out of us. And then sometime after midnight my other aunt Lottie in Australia rang. She'd switched on her phone to find loads of messages, and she was so concerned that she rang even though she knew that it would be well late here, and Mama took the phone outside again, and paced and paced and talked and talked, and then she came back to bed without bothering to shut the front door. And she forgot to lock the bedroom door as well, and I'm scared.'

'What are you scared of, Katia?'

'I'm scared that Granny might get up and start wandering again. I'm scared that she'll still be in witch mode.'

'May I remind you that you are owed Dream Time, Katia.'

'I am?'

'Yes. You have been owed Dream Time since the night Granny wet the bed. You didn't get a chance to talk to Tess then because Tess didn't sleep that night. It's coming up to Dream Time now, Katia. The sitting-room clock is about to chime three.'

Ding. Ding. Ding.

'Katia, this is the last favour the Dream Spinner can grant you. You must be very careful about how you choose to employ your time. Dreams are very precious. I wish you good luck.'

'Thank you, Charlotte.'

'The door of the Osier Pod is now open.'

'Is this the last time I'll be able to talk to you, Charlotte?'

'Yes, Katia.'

'I'm sorry to hear that. You have been a good friend to

187

me. It is not often that someone comes along who really and truly listens.'

'I'm touched. There will always be a special place in my heart for you, Katia.'

'Fare thee well, Charlotte!'

'Fare thee well, Katia!'

'Goodnight!'

'Goodnight!'

26

THE MERMAID'S SONG

The light's on in the sitting-room. There's a half-full wine glass on the table beside Mama's laptop. Displayed on the screen is a download of a tariff page. It's for a care home. Rates start from £750 a week.

The peacocks are crying in the garden down the road: I can hear them through the open front door. Outside, the gate is open too. Mama didn't close it when she came back from her walkabout because the primer was still tacky.

There's a full moon. The blossom on the cherry tree is silver. A light wind soughs through its branches; blossom falls, drifting onto the grass like gleaming confetti.

I go back into the house, into Granny's room, and sit down on the chair by her bed. I can tell by the rapid eye movement under her lids that she's deep in Dream Time.

'Hello,' I say.

'Who is it?' Her voice comes in the lisp that means that she doesn't have her teeth in.

'It's Katia, Granny.'

'Oh! Katia! How lovely! What are you doing here?'

'I'm watching over you, Granny.'

'Oh. Do I need watching over?'

'Oh, yes, indeed you do.'

'Why do I need watching over?'

'Because you're nearly ninety, and can't look after yourself.'

'I see. Someone wrote a song about that once, you know,' she says, conversationally. '"Someone to Watch Over Me". Shall I sing it for you?'

'Yes, do.'

'You might want to put your fingers in your ears. I was never much of a one for holding a tune.'

I laugh. 'Give it a go.'

'I'm shy, now.'

'Do the first verse.'

'You're sweet. You always were my favourite grandchild.' I don't bother to remind her that I'm her only grandchild. She smiles and shuts her eyes, and then, in a faltering voice, she starts singing, slowly and rather sweetly.

But I'm feeling antsy now. Like Charlotte said, Dream Time is precious, and I can't faff about.

I let her finish the first verse, and then she launches into the refrain.

'*Someone . . . to watch over me,*' she warbles 'That's you, Katia, I'm singing about. Isn't it? You're·the someone who's watching over me.'

'Yes, Granny. I am indeed. Now. Follow my lead, like it says in the song.' I'm all businesslike, like Mama when she's in carer mode.

'What do you mean?'

'Come with me.'

'You want me to get out of bed?'

'Yes.'

'But it's the middle of the night.'

'It's three o'clock in the morning. That's always the best time.'

'The best time for what?'

'For what we're going to do. Come on.'

'I haven't got my teeth in.'

'You won't need them where we're going.'

'Where are we going?'

'You'll find out when you get there. Just follow me.'

'I need help to get out of bed. Give me your hands.'

'No. You won't need help. You can do this by yourself. But don't worry. Because you know that I am here.'

Granny pulls back the covers and slides her stick legs out over the edge of the bed.

'Good Granny!' I tell her. 'Come on. I'll show you the way.'

'What about my cardigan? My slippers?'

'You won't need those either.'

'But you say I'm going out somewhere?'

'Yes.'

'Then let me at least put some lipstick on. I never go out anywhere without my lipstick, you know.' She pauses by the chest-of-drawers, reaches for her lipstick, applies it in a couple of strokes, then rubs her lips together. 'How's that?'

'Perfect, Granny. You look lovely.'

I lead the way, down the L-shaped corridor, through the front door, out into the sun porch. I look over my shoulder. She's walking doggedly, but this time there's no stump stump stump. 'You're doing great,' I tell her. 'See, I knew you could do it by yourself.'

Into the garden now, across the carpet of silvery blossom. I wait for Granny by the open gate. There are petals falling on her head; I think of the Selfish Giant lying in his garden, his dead body covered in blossom, his spirit alive and kicking in Paradise. It's not Paradise where Granny's going, but it sure as hell beats being possessed by a witch. She draws abreast of me and pauses. 'Where now?' she asks.

'Along there.' I point to the tunnel of trees that, in the daytime, casts such long shadows over the Gingerbread House.

'I suppose I'll have to do whatever you tell me to. Bossy boots.' She starts to move off along the road, then stops and looks back. 'Are you not coming?' she says.

'No, Granny. You have to do this bit on your own.'

'Why can't you come?'

'Because I've a job to do.'

'And what might that be?'

'I've to watch over Mama.'

'Oh, yes.' There's a pause. 'Katia?' she says.

'Yes?'

'You died, didn't you?'

'Yes, Granny. In a scuba-diving accident.'

'Oh, yes. I remember now. Was it in Jamaica?'

'No, it was off the Scottish Coast.'

'I'm sorry to hear about that.'

'No worries, Granny.'

'Shall I go now?'

'Yes.' I feel I ought to add something like 'your time has come', but it seems too melodramatic, somehow.

'Well. See you later, alligator.'

'In a while, crocodile. God speed.'

God speed. It's a comforting thing to say, isn't it, to someone who's setting off on a journey, whether or not you believe in a god? I watch Granny's retreating figure as she trudges off up the road, her mad, blossom-covered hair lambent in the moonlight. Lambent. That's another word Mama taught me. It means radiant. I'd better get back to Mama, but I'll wait until Granny's well and truly gone.

I wonder how the David Attenborough commentary would go, if this were one of his documentaries. 'Under the shadow of the trees she passes, singing one of her little ditties. As must happen to all our species, she's shuffling off her mortal coil at last, heading unerringly for the light at the end of the tunnel.'

I wonder what's going through Granny's head as she plods along the road. Maybe the light pollution from the city far on the horizon reminds her of the footlights in the theatres of her youth. Maybe she thinks she's taking a curtain call. I wish I could tell you that her demeanour changes, that her gait becomes more erect, that she glides gracefully away from life, but it doesn't happen like that. Her silhouette in her white flannelette nightdress just diminishes, gets smaller and smaller the further away she goes, and more and more shimmery, until I can't see her any more.

And now I know what Alice never did. I know what the flame of a candle looks like after the candle is blown out.

I turn back through the gate and move across the garden to the porch. I'll have to stand guard until the sun rises: I don't want to run the risk of any night-time passers-by investigating the Gingerbread House with its front door ajar, all lit up like an invitation to a burglar.

I sit down on the step and allow my mind to go back to my fourteenth birthday. A dive site on the west coast of Scotland.

★

Of course I'm not expecting the dive to be as special as the reefs in Jamaica, but as soon as I perform that backward roll and feel the sea churn around me in an explosion of bubbles and refracted silvery light, I feel more alive than I've ever been. I make the 'OK' signal to Mama and Dad, then draw a big smile across my face with my index finger. Mama and Dad smile back.

As we descend, bubbles fizzing from our regulators, I look around in a kind of trance. I know now how an addict might feel who had been denied a drug – I'm Pisces, back in my element!

Below us, the terrain looks as if it's been scattered with gold dust. Crabs covered in tattoos go about their business, scuttling across the sandy bottom, and starfish – ranging from the size of a dinner plate to the size of the nail on my pinkie finger – have bedecked themselves in pretty silken fronds. All around me are delicate, translucent jellyfish, and algae like giant pink powder puffs, and tubeworms glistening like jewels.

Tubeworms! They sound disgusting, don't they? But they're not. They're really, really pretty. Their homes are shaped like miniature angels' trumpets, and when they're all gathered together, they look like an arrangement in a posh florist's window. Every time you flick your fingers at them, they dive back into their little trumpet homes, and it's just like seeing the lights on a Christmas tree going on and off. And – oh! – you haven't lived until you've laughed at scallops in motion! They rise from the seabed when you prod them, and soar up through the water looking like Granny's false teeth chomping away randomly.

Mama and Dad and I frolic – it's the only word for it. Venting air, we descend further into a valley carpeted by brittlefish – tiny starfish whose filmy limbs float around them like feathery ribbons – and then Dad touches me lightly on the arm. I turn, and he points to the other side of the valley. About ten metres away I can just make out a dozen or so great streamlined shapes. Yikes! I turn to Dad and make the shark fin sign, hand rigid on my forehead, but he shakes his head, and I can see that his eyes are laughing behind his mask. He draws a smile across his face, then moves his right hand in a wavy, rhythmic way, mimicking the way dolphins move through the water. Dolphins! Oh, bliss! *Dolphins!* I'm nearly crying with happiness. I have never before been so brimful of feel-good endorphins as I watch the pod's graceful progress into the blue beyond. To judge by their comparative sizes there are about eight adults and three calves. Come back! Come back! I plead with my eyes. But their shapes slowly recede, disappearing like a vision in a dream.

I see Mama shrug – a gesture of regret – and then she taps on her gauge, reminding me to check my air. All that frolicking and laughing and oohing and aahing means that I've used up a fair bit, but I don't want to ascend – not just yet – so I make the OK sign, and we three frolic some more, until . . .

'It's definitely time to go up now,' Mama tells me, with a firm upwards jab of her thumb.

But 'hang on a minute', I tell her with my right hand. The legs of my dry suit are filling with excess air, and I need to perform the trick that vents it, otherwise I run the risk of making a feet-first ascent – not just terminally uncool, but dangerous, too. I tuck myself into a ball and quickly roll over on to my back, feeling the air rush to the exhaust valve on my arm. Yay! Chuffed I am, at my own niftiness.

'OK', I signal to Mama, and 'OK' I signal to Dad,

preparing myself to fin upward. But nothing happens. I breathe in deeply, hoping a good lungful of air will do the trick and help me ascend. Nope. I press the inflator valve to give my buoyancy a bit of a boost. *Nul points*, as Granny might say. I work my thigh muscles hard. Nothing. Then I decide to descend a little, so I can push myself off the bottom. Still nothing. *Nada. Zilch.*

I look at Mama, and wish I hadn't. Her eyes behind her mask are wide with concern, and her concern makes me fearful. 'Are you OK?' she signals, and I make the 'dodgy' sign back at her. *Take it easy*, Dad motions with his hand. *Stay calm. Everything's cool.* I try to breathe easy, but the breath I hear inside my head is ragged, coming and going in a rush as I snatch again and again at precious air. Dad reaches for my gauge to check the level, and I see his brow furrow. When he next looks at me, however, his eyes are all reassurance. He's putting on an act for my benefit, I know. He's trying to make sure I stay calm.

Dad moves around behind me, and in my peripheral vision I see him take his dive knife from the scabbard on his thigh. Looking up, I see fine lines of nylon waving to and fro in the current. My gear's entangled in fishing line. It must have happened when I did my backward roll. Don't panic, Katia, I tell myself. Stay calm. *Stay calm.* That's the rule that is reiterated on every single page of the chapter in the dive manual that deals with emergencies.

Dad's cutting through the tangled nylon, but it's taking too long. My gauge is dangerously low now. I know that the best way to help would be to allow myself to go limp, but panic is rising as fast as my air supply's being depleted, and I start to struggle, and pull at the nylon, entangling myself further.

196

Help! *Help!*

I'm wriggling; Dad's working away with his knife, and out of the corner of my eye I see that Mama's desperately signalling to me to share her air. No! I'm scared, too scared; my jaws tighten on the rubber between my teeth. I can't – won't – relinquish it. There's only one thing for it at this stage. Once free, I will have to make a runaway emergency ascent. I reach for the clasp on my weight belt. I wait. I wait. And I wait . . .

The last length of fishing line is slashed. Pulling at the release, I let the lead weights fall to the seabed, and then I'm freefalling in reverse, soaring to the surface, breathing out all the way because the first rule of scuba diving is *never hold your breath*. Above me the sun is dancing on the water, below me I see my parents' upturned white faces as they, too, ditch their belts and come hurtling up behind me. *Never hold your breath*. But I have none to hold. I'm clean out of air now, diving on empty.

I'm scuba girl Katia, beloved only child of Donn and Tess, saved from death by a neat Heimlich manoeuvre – and oh, how the sharp metal of that stupid Claddagh ring seared my windpipe! But this time the pain is much worse.

I'm Alice, falling down to Wonderland, chasing the White Rabbit, swimming in the pool of tears.

I'm the little mermaid off on her first adventure to the world above the waves, the world where the sun is a great ball of fiery light in the sky, and fish swim around the soughing branches of trees and sing to each other, and where a handsome prince with wavy brown hair and laughing green eyes is waiting for me. From far below, I hear my mer-family call 'god speed!' The sun is coming closer now, and any second I will pass through the glittering surface and pull sweet salt air into my lungs.

But . . .I . . .Don't . . .Make it.

★

It's dawn. The peacocks are clamouring in the garden down the road from the Gingerbread House. My fledgling blue tits will be chirping in their nest, poised to take flight and go frolic on their baby wings. And there's a song playing in my head.

It's the song a sentimental Mama used to play over the headphones when I was just a tiny baby floating inside her, the one the little mermaid sings about the world above the waves where the sun shines.

I can tell that Mama is dreaming when I get into bed beside her, so I slide into the dream and croon to her. I want to make her smile in her sleep.

Mama opens her eyes, but she's sleeping still. 'Katia?' she says.

'Yes, Mama?'

'Are you there?'

'Of course I'm here, Mama. I promised you I'd watch over you, didn't I? That's why I came with you, to the Gingerbread House. Katia keeps her promises.'

'You were – you *are* such a good girl. Oh, sweetheart, sweetheart – sometimes I don't know if you're here or if you're there, somewhere beyond in blue. You're such a good, good, beautiful girl.' She shuts her eyes again, and I see tears glistening on her lashes. 'Shall I tell you a story, my darling girl?'

'I'd love that.'

'Which one?'

'Which one do you think?'

'Your favourite?'

'My favourite.'

'Far out in the wide sea,' begins Mama, settling Teddy into the nook between her chin and collarbone, 'where the water is as blue as the loveliest cornflower, and where it is very, very deep, live the mer-people . . .'

ACKNOWLEDGEMENTS

Heartfelt thanks to the team at Black & White Publishing for their incredible support, kindness and vision: Campbell Brown, Alison McBride, Chris Kydd, Lina Langlee, Janne Moller, Daiden O'Regan, Thomas Ross, Henry Steadman and Debs Warner. It has been a tremendous pleasure to work with you all on *The Gingerbread House*. Huge thanks also to the team at Gill Hess and to Annabel Robinson and Sophie Goodfellow of FMcM Associates for their comradeship and acumen, and to my agent Margaret Halton for her wisdom. Cecelia Ahern, Roddy Doyle, Marian Keyes, Sue Leonard, Liz Nugent, Fiona O'Brien and Hilary Reynolds – in the words of E.B. White, 'It is not often someone comes along who is a true friend and a good writer.' A thousand thanks to bibliophile booksellers everywhere, with a special mention for Bob Johnston of my local bookshop, the Gutter.